WHOSE BODY?

When an architect discovers in his bath the dead body of a middle-aged stranger, wearing nothing but a pair of gold pince-nez, gentleman sleuth Lord Peter Wimsey is urged to investigate. Inspector Sugg is certain the corpse is that of the missing financier Sir Reuben Levy. Lord Peter is certain it is not. But there is undoubtedly a connection — for it seems someone wants them to *think* the dead man is Levy. Why would anyone construct such a grotesque tableau? Where is Levy now — alive or dead? And whose body *was* it in the bath?

Books by Dorothy L. Sayers
Published in Ulverscroft Collections:

CLOUDS OF WITNESS

DOROTHY L. SAYERS

WHOSE BODY?

A Lord Peter Wimsey Mystery

Complete and Unabridged

ULVERSCROFT
Leicester

First published in Great Britain in 1923 by
T. Fisher Unwin
London

First Ulverscroft Edition
published 2018
by arrangement with
Hodder & Stoughton
An Hachette UK company
London

To M. J.

Dear Jim,
This book is your fault. If it had not been for your brutal insistence, Lord Peter would never have staggered through to the end of this enquiry. Pray consider that he thanks you with his accustomed suavity.

Yours ever,
D. L. S.

1

'Oh damn!' said Lord Peter Wimsey at Piccadilly Circus. 'Hi, driver!'

The taxi man, irritated at receiving this appeal while negotiating the intricacies of turning into Lower Regent Street across the route of a 19 bus, a 38-B and a bicycle, bent an unwilling ear.

'I've left the catalogue behind,' said Lord Peter deprecatingly, 'uncommonly careless of me. D'you mind puttin' back to where we came from?'

'To the Savile Club, sir?'

'No — 110A Piccadilly — just beyond — thank you.'

'Thought you was in a hurry,' said the man, overcome with a sense of injury.

'I'm afraid it's an awkward place to turn in,' said Lord Peter, answering the thought rather than the words. His long, amiable face looked as if it had generated spontaneously from his top hat, as white maggots breed from Gorgonzola.

The taxi, under the severe eye of a policeman, revolved by slow jerks with a noise like the grinding of teeth.

The block of new, perfect and expensive flats in which Lord Peter dwelt upon the second floor, stood directly opposite the Green Park, in a spot for many years occupied by the skeleton of a frustrate commercial enterprise. As Lord

1

Peter let himself in he heard his man's voice in the library, uplifted in that throttled stridency peculiar to well-trained persons using the telephone.

'I believe that's his lordship just coming in again — if Your Grace would kindly hold the line a moment.'

'What is it, Bunter?'

'Her Grace has just called up from Denver, my lord. I was just saying your lordship had gone to the sale when I heard your lordship's latchkey.'

'Thanks,' said Lord Peter; 'and you might find me my catalogue, would you? I think I must have left it in my bedroom, or on the desk.'

He sat down to the telephone with an air of leisurely courtesy, as though it were an acquaintance dropped in for a chat.

'Hullo, Mother — that you?'

'Oh, there you are, dear,' replied the voice of the Dowager Duchess. 'I was afraid I'd just missed you.'

'Well, you had, as a matter of fact. I'd just started off to Brocklebury's sale to pick up a book or two, but I had to come back for the catalogue. What's up?'

'Such a quaint thing,' said the Duchess. 'I thought I'd tell you. You know little Mr Thipps?'

'Thipps?' said Lord Peter. 'Thipps? Oh, yes, the little architect man who's doing the church roof. Yes. What about him?'

'Mrs Throgmorton's just been in, in quite a state of mind.'

'Sorry, Mother, I can't hear. Mrs Who?'

2

'Throgmorton — Throgmorton — the vicar's wife.'

'Oh, Throgmorton, yes?'

'Mr Thipps rang them up this morning. It was his day to come down, you know.'

'Yes?'

'He rang them up to say he couldn't. He was so upset, poor little man. He'd found a dead body in his bath.'

'Sorry, Mother, I can't hear; found what, where?'

'A dead body, dear, in his bath.'

'What? — no, no, we haven't finished. Please don't cut us off. Hullo! Hullo! Is that you, Mother? Hullo! — Mother! — Oh yes — sorry, the girl was trying to cut us off. What sort of body?'

'A dead man, dear, with nothing on but a pair of pince-nez. Mrs Throgmorton positively blushed when she was telling me. I'm afraid people do get a little narrow-minded in country vicarages.'

'Well, it sounds a bit unusual. Was it anybody he knew?'

'No, dear, I don't think so, but, of course, he couldn't give her many details. She said he sounded quite distracted. He's such a respectable little man — and having the police in the house, and so on, really worried him.'

'Poor little Thipps! Uncommonly awkward for him. Let's see, he lives in Battersea, doesn't he?'

'Yes, dear; 59 Queen Caroline Mansions; opposite the Park. That big block just round the corner from the Hospital. I thought perhaps you'd like to run round and see him and ask if there's anything we can do. I always thought him a nice little man.'

'Oh, quite,' said Lord Peter, grinning at the telephone. The Duchess was always of the greatest assistance to his hobby of criminal investigation, though she never alluded to it, and maintained a polite fiction of its non-existence.

'What time did it happen, Mother?'

'I think he found it early this morning, but, of course, he didn't think of telling the Throgmortons just at first. She came up to me just before lunch — so tiresome, I had to ask her to stay. Fortunately, I was alone. I don't mind being bored myself, but I hate having my guests bored.'

'Poor old Mother! Well, thanks awfully for tellin' me. I think I'll send Bunter to the sale and toddle round to Battersea now an' try and console the poor little beast. So-long.'

'Good-bye, dear.'

'Bunter!'

'Yes, my lord.'

'Her Grace tells me that a respectable Battersea architect has discovered a dead man in his bath.'

'Indeed, my lord? That's very gratifying.'

'Very, Bunter. Your choice of words is unerring. I wish Eton and Balliol had done as much for me. Have you found the catalogue?'

'Here it is, my lord.'

'Thanks. I am going to Battersea at once. I want you to attend the sale for me. Don't lose

4

time — I don't want to miss the Folio Dante[1] nor the de Voragine — here you are — see? *Golden Legend* — Wynkyn de Worde, 1493 — got that? — and, I say, make a special effort for the Caxton folio of the *Four Sons of Aymon* — it's the 1489 folio and unique. Look! I've marked the lots I want, and put my outside offer against each. Do your best for me. I shall be back to dinner.'

'Very good, my lord.'

'Take my cab and tell him to hurry. He may for you; he doesn't like me very much. Can I,' said Lord Peter, looking at himself in the eighteenth-century mirror over the mantelpiece, 'can I have the heart to fluster the flustered Thipps further — that's very difficult to say quickly — by appearing in a top-hat and frock-coat? I think not. Ten to one he will overlook my trousers and mistake me for the undertaker. A grey suit, I fancy, neat but not gaudy, with a hat to tone suits my other self better. Exit the amateur of first editions; new

---

[1] This is the first Florence edition, 1481, by Niccolo di Lorenzo. Lord Peter's collection of printed Dantes is worth inspection. It includes, besides the famous Aldine 8vo of 1502, the Naples folio of 1477 — 'edizione rarissima,' according to Colomb. This copy has no history, and Mr Parker's private belief is that its present owner conveyed it away by stealth from somewhere or other. Lord Peter's own account is that he 'picked it up in a little place in the hills', when making a walking-tour through Italy.

5

motive introduced by solo bassoon; enter Sherlock Holmes, disguised as a walking gentleman. There goes Bunter. Invaluable fellow — never offers to do his job when you've told him to do somethin' else. Hope he doesn't miss the *Four Sons of Aymon*. Still, there *is* another copy of that — in the Vatican.[1] It might become available, you never know — if the Church of Rome went to pot or Switzerland invaded Italy — whereas a strange corpse doesn't turn up in a suburban bathroom more than once in a lifetime — at least, I should think not — at any rate, the number of times it's happened, *with* a pince-nez, might be counted on the fingers of one hand, I imagine. Dear me! it's a dreadful mistake to ride two hobbies at once.'

He had drifted across the passage into his bedroom, and was changing with a rapidity one might not have expected from a man of his mannerisms. He selected a dark-green tie to match his socks and tied it accurately without hesitation or the slightest compression of his lips; substituted a pair of brown shoes for his black ones, slipped a monocle into a breast pocket, and took up a beautiful Malacca walking-stick with a heavy silver knob.

'That's all, I think,' he murmured to himself. 'Stay — I may as well have you — you may come

---

[1] Lord Peter's wits were wool-gathering. The book is in the possession of Earl Spencer. The Brocklebury copy is incomplete, the last five signatures being altogether missing, but is unique in possessing the colophon.

6

in useful — one never knows.' He added a flat silver matchbox to his equipment, glanced at his watch, and seeing that it was already a quarter to three, ran briskly downstairs, and, hailing a taxi, was carried to Battersea Park.

Mr Alfred Thipps was a small, nervous man, whose flaxen hair was beginning to abandon the unequal struggle with destiny. One might say that his only really marked feature was a large bruise over the left eyebrow which gave him a faintly dissipated air incongruous with the rest of his appearance. Almost in the same breath with his first greeting, he made a self-conscious apology for it, murmuring something about having run against the dining-room door in the dark. He was touched almost to tears by Lord Peter's thoughtfulness and condescension in calling.

'I'm sure it's most kind of your lordship,' he repeated for the dozenth time, rapidly blinking his weak little eyelids. 'I appreciate it very deeply, very deeply, indeed, and so would Mother, only she's so deaf, I don't like to trouble you with making her understand. It's been very hard all day,' he added, 'with the policemen in the house and all this commotion. It's what Mother and me have never been used to, always living very retired, and it's most distressing to a man of regular habits, my lord, and reely, I'm almost thankful Mother doesn't understand, for I'm sure it would worry her terribly if she was to know about it. She was upset at first, but she's made up some idea of her own about it now, and I'm sure it's all for the best.'

The old lady who sat knitting by the fire nodded grimly in response to a look from her son.

'I always said as you ought to complain about that bath, Alfred,' she said suddenly, in the high, piping voice peculiar to the deaf, 'and it's to be 'oped the landlord'll see about it now; not but what I think you might have managed without having the police in, but there! you always were one to make a fuss about a little thing, from chicken-pox up.'

'There now,' said Mr Thipps apologetically, 'you see how it is. Not but what it's just as well she's settled on that, because she understands we've locked up the bathroom and don't try to go in there. But it's been a terrible shock to me, sir — my lord, I should say, but there! my nerves are all to pieces. Such a thing has never 'appened — happened to me in all my born days. Such a state I was in this morning — I didn't know if I was on my head or my heels — I reely didn't, and my heart not being too strong, I hardly knew how to get out of that horrid room and telephone for the police. It's affected me, sir, it's affected me, it reely has — I couldn't touch a bit of breakfast, nor lunch neither, and what with telephoning and putting off clients and inter- viewing people all morning, I've hardly known what to do with myself.'

'I'm sure it must have been uncommonly distressin',' said Lord Peter, sympathetically, 'especially comin' like that before breakfast. Hate anything tiresome happenin' before break- fast. Takes a man at such a confounded

8

disadvantage, what?'

'That's just it, that's just it,' said Mr Thipps, eagerly, 'when I saw that dreadful thing lying there in my bath, mother-naked, too, except for a pair of eyeglasses, I assure you, my lord, it regularly turned my stomach, if you'll excuse the expression. I'm not very strong, sir, and I get that sinking feeling sometimes in the morning, and what with one thing and another I'ad — had to send the girl for a stiff brandy, or I don't know *what* mightn't have happened. I felt so queer, though I'm anything but partial to spirits as a rule. Still, I make it a rule never to be without brandy in the house, in case of emergency, you know?'

'Very wise of you,' said Lord Peter, cheerfully, 'you're a very far-seein' man, Mr Thipps. Wonderful what a little nip'll do in case of need, and the less you're used to it the more good it does you. Hope your girl is a sensible young woman, what? Nuisance to have women faintin' and shriekin' all over the place.'

'Oh, Gladys is a good girl,' said Mr Thipps, 'very reasonable indeed. She was shocked, of course; that's very understandable. I was shocked myself, and it wouldn't be proper in a young woman not to be shocked under the circumstances, but she is reely a helpful, energetic girl in a crisis, if you understand me. I consider myself very fortunate these days to have got a good, decent girl to do for me and Mother, even though she is a bit careless and forgetful about little things, but that's only natural. She was very sorry indeed about having

9

left the bathroom window open, she reely was, and though I was angry at first, seeing what's come of it, it wasn't anything to speak of, not in the ordinary way, as you might say. Girls will forget things, you know, my lord, and reely she was so distressed I didn't like to say too much to her. All I said was: 'It might have been burglars,' I said, 'remember that, next time you leave a window open all night; this time it was a dead man,' I said, 'and that's unpleasant enough, but next time it might be burglars,' I said, 'and all of us murdered in our beds.' But the police-inspector — Inspector Sugg, they called him, from the Yard — he was very sharp with her, poor girl. Quite frightened her, and made her think he suspected her of something, though what good a body could be to her, poor girl, I can't imagine, and so I told the inspector. He was quite rude to me, my lord — I may say I didn't like his manner at all. 'If you've got anything definite to accuse Gladys or me of, Inspector,' I said to him, 'bring it forward, that's what you have to do,' I said, 'but I've yet to learn that you're paid to be rude to a gentleman in his own 'ouse — house.' Reely,' said Mr Thipps, growing quite pink on the top of his head, 'he regularly roused me, regularly roused me, my lord, and I'm a mild man as a rule.'

'Sugg all over,' said Lord Peter, 'I know him. When he don't know what else to say, he's rude. Stands to reason you and the girl wouldn't go collectin' bodies. Who'd want to saddle himself with a body? Difficulty's usually to get rid of 'em. Have you got rid of this one yet, by the way?'

'It's still in the bathroom,' said Mr Thipps. 'Inspector Sugg said nothing was to be touched till his men came in to move it. I'm expecting them at any time. If it would interest your lordship to have a look at it — '

'Thanks awfully,' said Lord Peter, 'I'd like to very much, if I'm not puttin' you out.'

'Not at all,' said Mr Thipps. His manner as he led the way along the passage convinced Lord Peter of two things — first, that, gruesome as his exhibit was, he rejoiced in the importance it reflected upon himself and his flat, and secondly, that Inspector Sugg had forbidden him to exhibit it to anyone. The latter supposition was confirmed by the action of Mr Thipps, who stopped to fetch the door-key from his bedroom, saying that he made it a rule to have two keys to every door, in case of accident.

The bathroom was in no way remarkable. It was long and narrow, the window being exactly over the head of the bath. The panes were of frosted glass; the frame wide enough to admit a man's body. Lord Peter stepped rapidly across to it, opened it and looked out.

The flat was the top one of the building and situated about the middle of the block. The bathroom window looked out upon the backyards of the flats, which were occupied by various small outbuildings, coal-holes, garages, and the like. Beyond these were the back gardens of a parallel line of houses. On the right rose the extensive edifice of St Luke's

Hospital, Battersea, with its grounds, and, connected with it by a covered way, the residence of the famous surgeon, Sir Julian Freke, who directed the surgical side of the great new hospital, and was, in addition, known in Harley Street as a distinguished neurologist with a highly individual point of view.

This information was poured into Lord Peter's ear at considerable length by Mr Thipps, who seemed to feel that the neighbourhood of anybody so distinguished shed a kind of halo of glory over Queen Caroline Mansions.

'We had him round here himself this morning,' he said, 'about this horrid business. Inspector Sugg thought one of the young medical gentlemen at the hospital might have brought the corpse round for a joke, as you might say, they always having bodies in the dissecting-room. So Inspector Sugg went round to see Sir Julian this morning to ask if there was a body missing. He was very kind, was Sir Julian, very kind indeed, though he was at work when they got there, in the dissecting-room. He looked up the books to see that all the bodies were accounted for, and then very obligingly came round here to look at this' — he indicated the bath — 'and said he was afraid he couldn't help us — there was no corpse missing from the hospital, and this one didn't answer to the description of any they'd had.'

'Nor to the description of any of the patients, I hope,' suggested Lord Peter casually.

At this grisly hint Mr Thipps turned pale.

'I didn't hear Inspector Sugg inquire,' he said,

with some agitation. 'What a very horrid thing that would be — God bless my soul, my lord, I never thought of it.'

'Well, if they had missed a patient they'd probably have discovered it by now,' said Lord Peter. 'Let's have a look at this one.'

He screwed his monocle into his eye, adding: 'I see you're troubled here with the soot blowing in. Beastly nuisance, ain't it? I get it, too — spoils all my books, you know. Here, don't you trouble, if you don't care about lookin' at it.'

He took from Mr Thipps's hesitating hand the sheet which had been flung over the bath, and turned it back.

The body which lay in the bath was that of a tall, stout man of about fifty. The hair, which was thick and black and naturally curly, had been cut and parted by a master hand, and exuded a faint violet perfume, perfectly recognisable in the close air of the bathroom. The features were thick, fleshy and strongly marked, with prominent dark eyes, and a long nose curving down to a heavy chin. The clean-shaven lips were full and sensual, and the dropped jaw showed teeth stained with tobacco. On the dead face the handsome pair of gold pince-nez mocked death with grotesque elegance; the fine gold chain curved over the naked breast. The legs lay stiffly stretched out side by side; the arms reposed close to the body; the fingers were flexed naturally. Lord Peter lifted one arm, and looked at the hand with a little frown.

'Bit of a dandy, your visitor, what?' he murmured. 'Parma violet and manicure.' He bent again, slipping his hand beneath the head. The absurd eyeglasses slipped off, clattering into the bath, and the noise put the last touch to Mr Thipps's growing nervousness.

'If you'll excuse me,' he murmured, 'it makes me feel quite faint, it reely does.'

He slipped outside, and he had no sooner done so than Lord Peter, lifting the body quickly and cautiously, turned it over and inspected it with his head on one side, bringing his monocle into play with the air of the late Joseph Chamberlain approving a rare orchid. He then laid the head over his arm, and bringing out the silver matchbox from his pocket, slipped it into the open mouth. Then making the noise usually written. 'Tut-tut,' he laid the body down, picked up the mysterious pince-nez, looked at it, put it on his nose and looked through it, made the same noise again, readjusted the pince-nez upon the nose of the corpse, so as to leave no traces of interference for the irritation of Inspector Sugg; rearranged the body; returned to the window and, leaning out, reached upwards and sideways with his walking-stick, which he had somewhat incongruously brought along with him. Nothing appearing to come of these investigations, he withdrew his head, closed the window, and rejoined Mr Thipps in the passage.

Mr Thipps, touched by this sympathetic interest in the younger son of a duke, took the liberty, on their return to the sitting-room, of offering him a cup of tea. Lord Peter, who had strolled over to the window and was admiring the outlook on Battersea Park, was about to accept, when an ambulance came into view at the end of Prince of Wales Road. Its appearance reminded Lord Peter of an important engagement, and with a hurried 'By Jove!' he took his leave of Mr Thipps.

'My mother sent kind regards and all that,' he said, shaking hands fervently; 'hopes you'll soon be down at Denver again. Good-bye, Mrs Thipps,' he bawled kindly into the ear of the old lady. 'Oh, no, my dear sir, please don't trouble to come down.'

He was none too soon. As he he stepped out of the door and turned towards the station, the ambulance drew up from the other direction, and Inspector Sugg emerged from it with two constables. The inspector spoke to the officer on duty at the Mansions, and turned a suspicious gaze on Lord Peter's retreating back.

'Dear old Sugg,' said that nobleman, fondly, 'dear, dear old bird! How he does hate me, to be sure.'

2

'Excellent, Bunter,' said Lord Peter, sinking with a sigh into a luxurious armchair. 'I couldn't have done better myself. The thought of the Dante makes my mouth water — and the *Four Sons of Aymon*. And you've saved me £60 — that's glorious. What shall we spend it on, Bunter? Think of it — all ours, to do as we like with, for as Harold Skimpole so rightly observes, £60 saved is £60 gained, and I'd reckoned on spending it all. It's your saving, Bunter, and properly speaking, your £60. What do we want? Anything in your department? Would you like anything altered in the flat?'

'Well, my lord, as your lordship is so good' — the manservant paused, about to pour an old brandy into a liqueur glass.

'Well, out with it, my Bunter, you imperturbable old hypocrite. It's no good talking as if you were announcing dinner — you're spilling the brandy. The voice is Jacob's voice, but the hands are the hands of Esau. What does that blessed darkroom of yours want now?'

'There's a Double Anastigmat with a set of supplementary lenses, my lord,' said Bunter, with a note almost of religious fervour. 'If it was a case of forgery now — or footprints — I could enlarge them right up on the plate. Or the wide-angled lens would be useful. It's as though the camera had eyes at the back of its head, my lord. Look — I've got it here.'

He pulled a catalogue from his pocket, and submitted it, quivering, to his employer's gaze.

Lord Peter perused the description slowly, the corners of his long mouth lifted into a faint smile.

'It's Greek to me,' he said, 'and £50 seems a ridiculous price for a few bits of glass. I suppose, Bunter, you'd say £750 was a bit out of the way for a dirty old book in a dead language, wouldn't you?'

'It wouldn't be my place to say so, my lord.'

'No, Bunter, I pay you £200 a year to keep your thoughts to yourself. Tell me, Bunter, in these democratic days, don't you think that's unfair?'

'No, my lord.'

'You don't. D'you mind telling me frankly why you don't think it unfair?'

'Frankly, my lord, your lordship is paid a nobleman's income to take Lady Worthington in to dinner and refrain from exercising your lordship's undoubted powers of repartee.'

Lord Peter considered this.

'That's your idea, is it, Bunter? *Noblesse oblige* — for a consideration. I daresay you're right. Then you're better off than I am, because I'd have to behave myself to Lady Worthington if I hadn't a penny. Bunter, if I sacked you here and now, would you tell me what you think of me?'

'No, my lord.'

'You'd have a perfect right to, my Bunter, and if I sacked you on top of drinking the kind of

17

coffee you make, I'd deserve everything you could say of me. You're a demon for coffee, Bunter — I don't know how you do it, because I believe it to be witchcraft, and I don't want to burn eternally. You can buy your cross-eyed lens.'

'Thank you, my lord.'

'Have you finished in the dining-room?'

'Not quite, my lord.'

'Well, come back when you have. I have many things to tell you. Hullo! who's that?'

The door bell had rung sharply.

'Unless it's anybody interestin' I'm not at home.'

'Very good, my lord.'

Lord Peter's library was one of the most delightful bachelor rooms in London. Its scheme was black and primrose; its walls were lined with rare editions, and its chairs and Chesterfield sofa suggested the embraces of the houris. In one corner stood a black baby-grand, a wood fire leaped on a wide old-fashioned hearth, and the Sevres vases on the chimney-piece were filled with ruddy and gold chrysanthemums. To the eyes of the young man who was ushered in from the raw November fog it seemed not only rare and unattainable, but friendly and familiar, like a colourful and gilded paradise in a mediaeval painting.

'Mr Parker, my lord.'

Lord Peter jumped up with genuine eagerness.

'My dear man, I'm delighted to see you. What a beastly foggy night, ain't it? Bunter, some more of that admirable coffee and another glass and the cigars. Parker, I hope you're full of crime — nothing less than arson or murder will do for us tonight. 'On such a night as this — ' Bunter and I were just sitting down to carouse. I've got a Dante, and a Caxton folio that is practically unique, at Sir Ralph Brocklebury's sale. Bunter, who did the bargaining, is going to have a lens which does all kinds of wonderful things with its eyes shut, and

We both have got a body in a bath,
We both have got a body in a bath —
   For in spite of all temptations
   To go in for cheap sensations
We insist upon a body in a bath —

Nothing less will do for us, Parker. It's mine at present, but we're going shares in it. Property of the firm. Won't you join us? You really must put *something* in the jackpot. Perhaps you have a body. Oh, do have a body. Everybody welcome.

Gin a body meet a body
   Hauled before the beak,
Gin a body jolly well knows who murdered
   a body and that old Sugg is on the wrong
   tack,
   Need a body speak?

Not a bit of it. He tips a glassy wink at yours truly and yours truly reads the truth.'
   'Ah,' said Parker. 'I knew you'd been round to Queen Caroline Mansions. So've I, and met Sugg, and he told me he'd seen you. He was cross, too.

19

Unwarrantable interference he calls it.'

'I knew he would,' said Lord Peter, 'I love taking a rise out of dear old Sugg, he's always so rude. I see by the *Star* that he has excelled himself by taking the girl, Gladys What's-her-name, into custody. Sugg of the evening, beautiful Sugg! But what were *you* doing there?'

'To tell you the truth,' said Parker, 'I went round to see if the Semitic-looking stranger in Mr Thipps's bath was by any extraordinary chance Sir Reuben Levy. But he isn't.'

'Sir Reuben Levy? Wait a minute, I saw something about that. I know! A headline: 'Mysterious disappearance of famous financier.' What's it all about? I didn't read it carefully.'

'Well, it's a bit odd, though I daresay it's nothing really — old chap may have cleared for some reason best known to himself. It only happened this morning, and nobody would have thought anything about it, only it happened to be the day on which he had arranged to attend a most important financial meeting and do some deal involving millions — I haven't got all the details. But I know he's got enemies who'd just as soon the deal didn't come off, so when I got wind of this fellow in the bath, I buzzed round to have a look at him. It didn't seem likely, of course, but unlikelier things do happen in our profession. The funny thing is, old Sugg has got bitten with the idea it *is* him, and is wildly telegraphing to Lady Levy to come and identify him. But as a matter of fact, the man in the bath is no more Sir Reuben Levy than Adolf Beck, poor devil, was John Smith. Oddly enough,

20

though, he would be really extraordinarily like Sir Reuben if he had a beard, and as Lady Levy is abroad with the family, somebody may say it's him, and Sugg will build up a lovely theory, like the Tower of Babel, and destined so to perish.'

'Sugg's a beautiful, braying ass,' said Lord Peter. 'He's like a detective in a novel. Well, I don't know anything about Levy, but I've seen the body, and I should say the idea was preposterous upon the face of it. What do you think of the brandy?'

'Unbelievable, Wimsey — sort of thing makes one believe in heaven. But I want your yarn.'

'D'you mind if Bunter hears it, too? Invaluable man, Bunter — amazin' fellow with a camera. And the odd thing is, he's always on the spot when I want my bath or my boots. I don't know when he develops things — I believe he does 'em in his sleep. Bunter!'

'Yes, my lord.'

'Stop fiddling about in there, and get yourself the proper things to drink and join the merry throng.'

'Certainly, my lord.'

'Mr Parker has a new trick: The Vanishing Financier. Absolutely no deception. Hey, presto, pass! and where is he? Will some gentleman from the audience kindly step upon the platform and inspect the cabinet? Thank you, sir. The quickness of the 'and deceives the heye.'

'I'm afraid mine isn't much of a story,' said Parker. 'It's just one of those simple things that offer no handle. Sir Reuben Levy dined last

21

night with three friends at the Ritz. After dinner the friends went to the theatre. He refused to go with them on account of an appointment. I haven't yet been able to trace the appointment, but anyhow, he returned home to his house — 9A Park Lane — at twelve o'clock.'

'Who saw him?'

'The cook, who had just gone up to bed, saw him on the doorstep, and heard him let himself in. He walked upstairs, leaving his greatcoat on the hall peg and his umbrella in the stand — you remember how it rained last night. He undressed and went to bed. Next morning he wasn't there. That's all,' said Parker abruptly, with a wave of the hand.

'It isn't all, it isn't all. Daddy, go on, that's not *half* a story,' pleaded Lord Peter.

'But it *is* all. When his man came to call him he wasn't there. The bed had been slept in. His pyjamas and all his clothes were there, the only odd thing being that they were thrown rather untidily on the ottoman at the foot of the bed, instead of being folded on a chair, as is Sir Reuben's custom — looking as though he had been rather agitated or unwell. No clean clothes were missing, no suit, no boots — nothing. The boots he had worn were in his dressing-room as usual. He had washed and cleaned his teeth and done all the usual things. The housemaid was down cleaning the hall at half-past six, and can swear that nobody came in or out after that. So one is forced to suppose that a respectable middle-aged Hebrew financier either went mad between twelve and six a.m. and walked quietly out of the house in his birthday suit on a November night, or else was spirited away like the lady in the *Ingoldsby Legends*, body and bones, leaving only a heap of crumpled clothes behind him.'

'Was the front door bolted?'

'That's the sort of question you *would* ask, straight off; it took me an hour to think of it. No; contrary to custom, there was only the Yale lock on the door. On the other hand, some of the maids had been given leave to go to the theatre, and Sir Reuben may quite conceivably have left the door open under the impression they had not come in. Such a thing has happened before.'

'And that's really all?'

'Really all. Except for one very trifling circumstance.'

'I love trifling circumstances,' said Lord Peter, with childish delight; 'so many men have been hanged by trifling circumstances. What was it?'

'Sir Reuben and Lady Levy, who are a most devoted couple, always share the same room. Lady Levy, as I said before, is in Mentone at the moment for her health. In her absence, Sir Reuben sleeps in the double bed as usual, and invariably on his own side — the outside — of the bed. Last night he put the two pillows together and slept in the middle, or, if anything, rather closer to the wall than otherwise. The housemaid, who is a most intelligent girl, noticed this when she went up to make the bed, and, with really admirable detective instinct, refused to touch the bed or

23

let anybody else touch it, though it wasn't till later that they actually sent for the police.'

'Was nobody in the house but Sir Reuben and the servants?'

'No; Lady Levy was away with her daughter and her maid. The valet, cook, parlourmaid, housemaid and kitchenmaid were the only people in the house, and naturally wasted an hour or two squawking and gossiping. I got there about ten.'

'What have you been doing since?'

'Trying to get on the track of Sir Reuben's appointment last night, since, with the exception of the cook, his 'appointer' was the last person who saw him before his disappearance. There may be some quite simple explanation, though I'm dashed if I can think of one for the moment. Hang it all, a man doesn't come in and go to bed and walk away again 'mid nodings on' in the middle of the night.'

'He may have been disguised.'

'I thought of that — in fact, it seems the only possible explanation. But it's deuced odd, Wimsey. An important City man, on the eve of an important transaction, without a word of warning to anybody, slips off in the middle of the night, disguised down to his skin, leaving behind his watch, purse, cheque-book, and — most mysterious and important of all — his spectacles, without which he can't see a step, as he is extremely short-sighted. He — '

'That *is* important,' interrupted Wimsey. 'You are sure he didn't take a second pair?'

'His man vouches for it that he had only two

24

pairs, one of which was found on his dressing-table, and the other in the drawer where it is always kept.'

Lord Peter whistled.

'You've got me there, Parker. Even if he'd gone out to commit suicide he'd have taken those.'

'So you'd think — or the suicide would have happened the first time he started to cross the road. However, I didn't overlook the possibility. I've got particulars of all today's street accidents, and I can lay my hand on my heart and say that none of them is Sir Reuben. Besides, he took his latch-key with him, which looks as though he'd meant to come back.'

'Have you seen the men he dined with?'

'I found two of them at the club. They said that he seemed in the best of health and spirits, spoke of looking forward to joining Lady Levy later on — perhaps at Christmas — and referred with great satisfaction to this morning's business transaction, in which one of them — a man called Anderson of Wyndham's — was himself concerned.'

'Then up till about nine o'clock, anyhow, he had no apparent intention or expectation of disappearing.'

'None — unless he was a most consummate actor. Whatever happened to change his mind must have happened either at the mysterious appointment which he kept after dinner, or while he was in bed between midnight and 5.30 a.m.'

'Well, Bunter,' said Lord Peter, 'what do you make of it?'

25

'Not in my department, my lord. Except that it is odd that a gentleman who was too flurried or unwell to fold his clothes as usual should remember to clean his teeth and put his boots out. Those are two things that quite frequently get overlooked, my lord.'

'If you mean anything personal, Bunter,' said Lord Peter, 'I can only say that I think the speech an unworthy one. It's a sweet little problem, Parker mine. Look here, I don't want to butt in, but I should dearly love to see that bedroom tomorrow. 'Tis not that I mistrust thee, dear, but I should uncommonly like to see it. Say me not nay — take another drop of brandy and a Villar y Villar, but say not, say not nay!'

'Of course you can come and see it — you'll probably find lots of things I've overlooked,' said the other, equably, accepting the proffered hospitality.

'Parker, acushla, you're an honour to Scotland Yard. I look at you, and Sugg appears a myth, a fable, an idiot-boy, spawned in a moonlight hour by some fantastic poet's brain. Sugg is too perfect to be possible. What does he make of the body, by the way?'

'Sugg says,' replied Parker, with precision. 'that the body died from a blow on the back of the neck. The doctor told him that. He says it's been dead a day or two. The doctor told him that, too. He says it's the body of a well-to-do Hebrew of about fifty. Anybody could have told him that. He says it's ridiculous to suppose it came in through the window without anybody knowing anything about it. He says it probably

26

walked in through the front door and was murdered by the household. He's arrested the girl because she's short and frail-looking and quite unequal to downing a tall and sturdy Semite with a poker. He'd arrest Thipps, only Thipps was away in Manchester all yesterday and the day before and didn't come back till late last night — in fact, he wanted to arrest him till I reminded him that if the body had been a day or two dead, little Thipps couldn't have done him in at 10.30 last night. But he'll arrest him tomorrow as an accessory — and the old lady with the knitting, too, I shouldn't wonder.'

'Well, I'm glad the little man has so much of an alibi,' said Lord Peter, 'though if you're only gluing your faith to cadaveric lividity, rigidity, and all the other quiddities, you must be prepared to have some sceptical beast of a prosecuting counsel walk slap-bang through the medical evidence. Remember Impey Biggs defending in that Chelsea teashop affair? Six bloomin' medicos contradictin' each other in the box, an' old Impey elocutin' abnormal cases from Glaister and Dixon Mann till the eyes of the jury reeled in their heads! 'Are you prepared to swear, Dr Thingumtight, that the onset of *rigor mortis* indicates the hour of death without the possibility of error?' 'So far as my experience goes, in the majority of cases,' says the doctor, all stiff. 'Ah!' says Biggs, 'but this is a Court of Justice, Doctor, not a Parliamentary election. We can't get on without a minority report. The law, Dr Thingumtight, respects the rights of the minority, alive or dead.' Some ass laughs, and old Biggs sticks his chest out and gets impressive. 'Gentlemen, this is no laughing matter. My client — an upright and honourable gentleman — is being tried for his life — for his life, gentlemen — and it is the business of the prosecution to show his guilt — if they can — without a shadow of doubt. Now, Dr Thingumtight, I ask you again, can you solemnly swear, without the least shadow of doubt — probable, possible shadow of doubt — that this unhappy woman met her death neither sooner nor later than Thursday evening? A probable opinion? Gentlemen, we are not Jesuits, we are straightforward Englishmen. You cannot ask a British-born jury to convict any man on the authority of a probable opinion.' Hum of applause.'

'Biggs' man was guilty all the same,' said Parker.

'Of course he was. But he was acquitted all the same, an' what you've just said is libel,' Wimsey walked over to the bookshelf and took down a volume of *Medical Jurisprudence* ''Rigor mortis — can only be stated in a very general way — many factors determine the result.' Cautious brute. 'On the average, however, stiffening will have begun — neck and jaw — 5 to 6 hours after death' — m'm — 'in all likelihood have passed off in the bulk of cases by the end of 36 hours. Under certain circumstances, however, it may appear unusually early, or be retarded unusually long!' Helpful, ain't it, Parker? 'Brown-Séquard states . . . 3½ minutes after death . . . In certain cases not until lapse of 16 hours after death

. . . present as long as 21 days thereafter.' Lord! 'Modifying factors — age — muscular state — or febrile diseases — or where temperature of environment is high' — and so on and so on — any bloomin' thing. Never mind. You can run the argument for what it's worth to Sugg. *He* won't know any better.' He tossed the book away. 'Come back to facts. What did *you* make of the body?'

'Well,' said the detective, 'not very much — I was puzzled — frankly. I should say he had been a rich man, but self-made, and that his good fortune had come to him fairly recently.'

'Ah, you noticed the calluses on the hands — I thought you wouldn't miss that.'

'Both his feet were badly blistered — he had been wearing tight shoes.'

'Walking a long way in them, too,' said Lord Peter, 'to get such blisters as that. Didn't that strike you as odd, in a person evidently well off?'

'Well, I don't know. The blisters were two or three days old. He might have got stuck in the suburbs one night, perhaps — last train gone and no taxi — and had to walk home.'

'Possibly.'

'There were some little red marks all over his back and one leg I couldn't quite account for.'

'I saw them.'

'What did you make of them?'

'I'll tell you afterwards. Go on.'

'He was very long-sighted — oddly long-sighted for a man in the prime of life; the glasses were like a very old man's. By the way, they had a very beautiful and remarkable chain of flat

29

links chased with a pattern. It struck me he might be traced through it.'

'I've just put an advertisement in The Times about it,' said Lord Peter. 'Go on.'

'He had had the glasses some time — they had been mended twice.'

'Beautiful, Parker, beautiful. Did you realise the importance of that?'

'Not specially, I'm afraid — why?'

'Never mind — go on.'

'He was probably a sullen, ill-tempered man — his nails were filed down to the quick as though he habitually bit them, and his fingers were bitten as well. He smoked quantities of cigarettes without a holder. He was particular about his personal appearance.'

'Did you examine the room at all? I didn't get a chance.'

'I couldn't find much in the way of footprints. Sugg & Co. had tramped all over the place, to say nothing of little Thipps and the maid, but I noticed a very definite patch just behind the head of the bath, as though something damp might have stood there. You could hardly call it a print.'

'It rained hard all last night, of course.'

'Yes; did you notice that the soot on the window-sill was vaguely marked?'

'I did,' said Wimsey, 'and I examined it hard with this little fellow, but I could make nothing of it except that something or other had rested on the sill.' He drew out his monocle and handed it to Parker.

'My word, that's a powerful lens.'

'It is,' said Wimsey, 'and jolly useful when you want to take a good squint at somethin' and look like a bally fool all the time. Only it don't do to wear it permanently — if people see you full-face they say: 'Dear me! how weak the sight of that eye must be!' Still, it's useful.'

'Sugg and I explored the ground at the back of the building,' went on Parker, 'but there wasn't a trace.'

'That's interestin'. Did you try the roof?'

'No.'

'We'll go over it tomorrow. The gutter's only a couple of feet off the top of the window. I measured it with my stick — the gentleman-scout's vade mecum, I call it — it's marked off in inches. Uncommonly handy companion at times. There's a sword inside and a compass in the head. Got it made specially. Anything more?'

'Afraid not. Let's hear your version, Wimsey.'

'Well, I think you've got most of the points. There are just one or two little contradictions. For instance, here's a man wears expensive gold-rimmed pince-nez and has had them long enough to be mended twice. Yet his teeth are not merely discoloured, but badly decayed and look as if he'd never cleaned them in his life. There are four molars missing on one side and three on the other and one front tooth broken right across. He's a man careful of his personal appearance, as witness his hair and his hands. What do you say to that?'

'Oh, these self-made men of low origin don't think much about teeth, and are terrified of dentists.'

31

'True; but one of the molars has a broken edge so rough that it had made a sore place on the tongue. Nothing's more painful. D'you mean to tell me a man would put up with that if he could afford to get the tooth filed?'

'Well, people are queer. I've known servants endure agonies rather than step over a dentist's door-mat. How did you see that, Wimsey?'

'Had a look inside; electric torch,' said Lord Peter. 'Handy little gadget. Looks like a matchbox. Well — I daresay it's all right, but I just draw your attention to it. Second point: Gentleman with hair smellin' of Parma violet and manicured hands and all the rest of it, never washes inside his ears. Full of wax. Nasty.'

'You've got me there, Wimsey; I never noticed it. Still — old bad habits die hard.'

'Right oh! Put it down at that. Third point: Gentleman with the manicure and the brilliantine and all the rest of it suffers from fleas.'

'By Jove, you're right! Flea-bites. It never occurred to me.'

'No doubt about it, old son. The marks were faint and old, but unmistakable.'

'Of course, now you mention it. Still, that might happen to anybody. I loosed a whopper in the best hotel in Lincoln the week before last. I hope it bit the next occupier!'

'Oh, all these things *might* happen to anybody — separately. Fourth point: Gentleman who uses Parma violet for his hair, etc., etc., washes his body in strong carbolic soap — so strong that the smell hangs about twenty-four hours later.'

'Carbolic to get rid of the fleas.'

'I will say for you, Parker, you've an answer for everything. Fifth point: Carefully got-up gentleman, with manicured, though masticated, finger-nails, has filthy black toe-nails which look as if they hadn't been cut for years.'

'All of a piece with habits as indicated.'

'Yes, I know, but such habits! Now, sixth, and last point: This gentleman with the intermittently gentlemanly habits arrives in the middle of a pouring wet night, and apparently through the window, when he has already been twenty-four hours dead, and lies down quietly in Mr Thipps's bath, unseasonably dressed in a pair of pince-nez. Not a hair on his head is ruffled — the hair has been cut so recently that there are quite a number of little short hairs stuck on his neck and the sides of the bath — and he has shaved so recently that there is a line of dried soap on his cheek — '

'Wimsey!'

'Wait a minute — and *dried soap in his mouth.*'

Bunter got up and appeared suddenly at the detective's elbow, the respectful man-servant all over.

'A little more brandy, sir?' he murmured.

'Wimsey,' said Parker, 'you are making me feel cold all over.' He emptied his glass — stared at it as though he were surprised to find it empty, set it down, got up, walked across to the bookcase, turned round, stood with his back against it and said:

'Look here, Wimsey — you've been reading detective stories, you're talking nonsense.'

33

'No, I ain't,' said Lord Peter, sleepily, 'uncommon good incident for a detective story, though, what? Bunter, we'll write one, and you shall illustrate it with photographs.'

'Soap in his — Rubbish!' said Parker. 'It was something else — some discolouration — '

'No,' said Lord Peter, 'there were hairs as well. Bristly ones. He had a beard.'

He took his watch from his pocket, and drew out a couple of longish, stiff hairs, which he had imprisoned between the inner and the outer case.

Parker turned them over once or twice in his fingers, looked at them close to the light, examined them with a lens, handed them to the impassible Bunter, and said:

'Do you mean to tell me, Wimsey, that any man alive would' — he laughed harshly — 'shave off his beard with his mouth open, and then go and get killed with his mouth full of hairs? You're mad.'

'I don't tell you so,' said Wimsey. 'You policemen are all alike — only one idea in your skulls. Blest if I can make out why you're ever appointed. He was shaved after he was dead. Pretty, ain't it? Uncommonly jolly little job for the barber, what? Here, sit down, man, and don't be an ass, stumpin' about the room like that. Worse things happen in war. This is only a blinkin' old shillin' shocker. But I'll tell you what, Parker, we're up against a criminal — *the* criminal — the real artist and blighter with imagination — real, artistic, finished stuff. I'm enjoying this, Parker.'

34

3

Lord Peter finished a Scarlatti sonata, and sat looking thoughtfully at his own hands. The fingers were long and muscular, with wide, flat joints and square tips. When he was playing his rather hard grey eyes softened, and his long, indeterminate mouth hardened in compensation. At no other time had he any pretentions to good looks, and at all times he was spoilt by a long, narrow chin, and a long, receding forehead, accentuated by the brushed-back sleekness of his tow-coloured hair. Labour papers, softening down the chin, caricatured him as a typical aristocrat.

'That's a wonderful instrument,' said Parker.

'It ain't so bad,' said Lord Peter, 'but Scarlatti wants a harpsichord. Piano's too modern — all thrills and overtones. No good for our job, Parker. Have you come to any conclusion?'

'The man in the bath,' said Parker, methodically, 'was *not* a well-off man careful of his personal appearance. He was a labouring man, unemployed, but who had only recently lost his employment. He had been tramping about looking for a job when he met with his end. Somebody killed him and washed him and scented him and shaved him in order to disguise him, and put him into Thipps's bath without leaving a trace. Conclusion: the murderer was a powerful man, since he killed him with a single blow on the neck, a man of cool head and masterly intellect, since he did all that ghastly business without leaving a mark, a man of wealth and refinement, since he had all the apparatus of an elegant toilet handy, and a man of bizarre, and almost perverted imagination, as is shown in the two horrible touches of putting the body in the bath and of adorning it with a pair of pince-nez.'

'He is a poet of crime,' said Wimsey. 'By the way, your difficulty about the pince-nez is cleared up. Obviously, the pince-nez never belonged to the body.'

'That only makes a fresh puzzle. One can't suppose the murderer left them in that obliging manner as a clue to his own identity.'

'We can hardly suppose that: I'm afraid this man possessed what most criminals lack — a sense of humour.'

'Rather macabre humour.'

'True. But a man who can afford to be humorous at all in such circumstances is a terrible fellow. I wonder what he did with the body between the murder and depositing it *chez.* Thipps. Then there are more questions. How did he get it there? And why? Was it brought in at the door, as Sugg of our heart suggests? or through the window, as we think, on the not very adequate testimony of a smudge on the window-sill? Had the murderer accomplices? Is little Thipps really in it, or the girl? It don't do to put the notion out of court merely because Sugg inclines to it. Even idiots occasionally speak the truth accidentally. If not, why was Thipps

36

selected for such an abominable practical joke? Has anybody got a grudge against Thipps? Who are the people in the other flats? We must find out that. Does Thipps play the piano at midnight over their heads or damage the reputation of the staircase by bringing home dubiously respectable ladies? Are there unsuccessful architects thirsting for his blood? Damn it all, Parker, there must be a motive somewhere. Can't have a crime without a motive, you know.'

'A madman — ' suggested Parker, doubtfully.

'With a deuced lot of method in his madness. He hasn't made a mistake — not one, unless leaving hairs in the corpse's mouth can be called a mistake. Well, anyhow, it's not Levy — you're right there. I say, old thing, neither your man nor mine has left much clue to go upon, has he? And there don't seem to be any motives knockin' about, either. And we seem to be two suits of clothes short in last night's work. Sir Reuben makes tracks without so much as a fig-leaf, and a mysterious individual turns up with a pince-nez, which is quite useless for purposes of decency. Dash it all! If only I had some good excuse for takin' up this body case officially — '

The telephone bell rang. The silent Bunter, whom the other two had almost forgotten, padded across to it.

'It's an elderly lady, my lord,' he said, 'I think she's deaf — I can't make her hear anything, but she's asking for your lordship.'

Lord Peter seized the receiver, and yelled into it a 'Hello!' that might have cracked the vulcanite. He listened for some minutes with an incredulous smile, which gradually broadened into a grin of delight. At length he screamed: 'All right! all right!' several times, and rang off.

'By Jove!' he announced, beaming, 'sportin' old bird! It's old Mrs Thipps. Deaf as a post. Never used the phone before. But determined. Perfect Napoleon. The incomparable Sugg has made a discovery and arrested little Thipps. Old lady abandoned in the flat. Thipps's last shriek to her: 'Tell Lord Peter Wimsey.' Old girl undaunted. Wrestles with telephone book. Wakes up the people at the exchange. Won't take no for an answer (not bein' able to hear it), gets through, says: 'Will I do what I can?' Says she would feel safe in the bands of a real gentleman. Oh, Parker, Parker! I could kiss her, I reely could, as Thipps says. I'll write to her instead — no, hang it, Parker, we'll go round. Bunter, get your infernal machine and the magnesium. I say, we'll go into partnership — pool the two cases and work 'em out together. You shall see my body tonight, Parker, and I'll look for your wandering Jew tomorrow. I feel so happy, I shall explode. O Sugg, Sugg, how art thou suggified! Bunter, my shoes. I say, Parker, I suppose yours are rubber-soled. Not? Tut, tut, you mustn't go out like that. We'll lend you a pair. Gloves? Here. My stick, my torch, the lampblack, the forceps, knife, pill-boxes — all complete?'

'Certainly, my lord.'

'Oh, Bunter, don't look so offended. I mean no harm. I believe in you, I trust you — what money have I got? That'll do. I knew a man once, Parker, who let a world-famous poisoner slip through his fingers, because the machine on the Underground took nothing but pennies. There was a queue at the booking office and the man at the barrier stopped him, and while they were arguing about accepting a five-pound-note (which was all he had) for a twopenny ride to Baker Street, the criminal had sprung into a Circle train, and was next heard of in Constantinople, disguised as an elderly Church of England clergyman touring with his niece. Are we all ready? Go!'

They stepped out, Bunter carefully switching off the lights behind them.

★ ★ ★

As they emerged into the gloom and gleam of Piccadilly, Wimsey stopped short with a little exclamation.

'Wait a second,' he said, 'I've thought of something. If Sugg's there he'll make trouble. I must short-circuit him.'

He ran back, and the other two men employed a few minutes of his absence in capturing a taxi.

Inspector Sugg and a subordinate Cerberus were on guard at 59 Queen Caroline Mansions, and showed no disposition to admit unofficial inquirers. Parker, indeed, they could not easily turn away, but Lord Peter found himself confronted with a surly manner and what Lord Beaconsfield described as a masterly inactivity. It was in vain that Lord Peter pleaded that he had been retained by Mrs Thipps on behalf of her son.

39

'Retained!' said Inspector Sugg, with a snort, 'she'll be retained if she doesn't look out. Shouldn't wonder if she wasn't in it herself, only she's so deaf, she's no good for anything at all.'

'Look here, Inspector,' said Lord Peter, 'what's the use of bein' so bally obstructive? You'd much better let me in — you know I'll get there in the end. Dash it all, it's not as if I was takin' the bread out of your children's mouths. Nobody paid me for finding Lord Attenbury's emeralds for you.'

'It's my duty to keep out the public,' said Inspector Sugg, morosely, 'and it's going to stay out.'

'I never said anything about your keeping out of the public,' said Lord Peter, easily, sitting down on the staircase to thrash the matter out comfortably, 'though I've no doubt pussy-foot's a good thing, on principle, if not exaggerated. The golden mean, Sugg, as Aristotle says, keeps you from bein' a golden ass. Ever been a golden ass, Sugg? I have. It would take a whole rose-garden to cure me, Sugg —

You are my garden of beautiful roses,
My own rose, my one rose, that's you!'

'I'm not going to stay any longer talking to you,' said the harassed Sugg, 'it's bad enough — hullo, drat that telephone. Here, Cawthorn, go and see what it is, if that old catamaran will let you into the room. Shutting herself up there and screaming,' said the inspector, 'it's enough to make a man give up crime and take to hedging and ditching.'

The constable came back:

'It's from the Yard, sir,' he said, coughing apologetically, 'the Chief says every facility is to be given to Lord Peter Wimsey, sir. Um!' He stood apart non-committally, glazing his eyes.

'Five aces,' said Lord Peter, cheerfully. 'The Chief's a dear friend of my mother's. No go, Sugg, it's no good buckin' you've got a full house. I'm goin' to make it a bit fuller.'

He walked in with his followers.

The body had been removed a few hours previously, and when the bathroom and the whole flat had been explored by the naked eye and the camera of the competent Bunter, it became evident that the real problem of the household was old Mrs Thipps. Her son and servant had both been removed, and it appeared that they had no friends in town, beyond a few business acquaintances of Thipps's, whose very addresses the old lady did not know. The other flats in the building were occupied respectively by a family of seven, at present departed to winter abroad, an elderly Indian colonel of ferocious manners, who lived alone with an Indian man-servant, and a highly respectable family on the third floor, whom the disturbance over their heads had outraged to the last degree. The husband, indeed, when appealed to by Lord Peter, showed a little human weakness, but Mrs Appledore, appearing suddenly in a warm dressing-gown, extricated him from the difficulties into which he was carelessly wandering.

'I am sorry,' she said, 'I'm afraid we can't

41

interfere in any way. This is a very unpleasant business, Mr — I'm afraid I didn't catch your name, and we have always found it better not to be mixed up with the police. Of course, *if* the Thippses are innocent, and I am sure I hope they are, it is very unfortunate for them, but I must say that the circumstances seem to me most suspicious, and to Theophilus too, and I should not like to have it said that we had assisted murderers. We might even be supposed to be accessories. Of course you are young, Mr — '

'This is Lord Peter Wimsey, my dear,' said Theophilus mildly.

She was unimpressed.

'Ah, yes,' she said, 'I believe you are distantly related to my late cousin, the Bishop of Carisbrooke. Poor man! He was always being taken in by impostors; he died without ever learning any better. I imagine you take after him, Lord Peter.'

'I doubt it,' said Lord Peter. 'So far as I know he is only a connection, though it's a wise child that knows its own father. I congratulate you, dear lady, on takin' after the other side of the family. You'll forgive my buttin' in upon you like this in the middle of the night, though, as you say, it's all in the family, and I'm sure I'm very much obliged to you, and for permittin' me to admire that awfully fetchin' thing you've got on. Now, don't you worry, Mr Appledore. I'm thinkin' the best thing I can do is to trundle the old lady down to my mother and take her out of your way, otherwise you might be findin' your

Christian feelin's gettin' the better of you some fine day, and there's nothin' like Christian feelin's for upsettin' a man's domestic comfort. Good-night, sir — good-night, dear lady — it's simply rippin' of you to let me drop in like this.'

'Well!' said Mrs Appledore, as the door closed behind him.

And —

> *'I thank the goodness and the grace*
> *That on my birth have smiled'*

said Lord Peter, 'and taught me to be bestially impertinent when I choose. Cat!'

Two a.m. saw Lord Peter Wimsey arrive in a friend's car at the Dower House, Denver Castle, in company with a deaf and aged lady and an antique portmanteau.

★ ★ ★

'It's very nice to see you, dear,' said the Dowager Duchess, placidly. She was a small, plump woman, with perfectly white hair and exquisite hands. In feature she was as unlike her second son as she was like him in character; her black eyes twinkled cheerfully, and her manners and movements were marked with a neat and rapid decision. She wore a charming wrap from Liberty's, and sat watching Lord Peter eat cold beef and cheese as though his arrival in such incongruous circumstances and company were the most ordinary event possible, which with him, indeed, it was.

43

'Have you got the old lady to bed?' asked Lord Peter.

'Oh, yes, dear. Such a striking old person, isn't she? And very courageous. She tells me she has never been in a motor-car before. But she thinks you a very nice lad, dear — that careful of her, you remind her of her own son. Poor little Mr Thipps — whatever made your friend the inspector think he could have murdered anybody?'

'My friend the inspector — no, no more, thank you, Mother — is determined to prove that the intrusive person in Thipps's bath is Sir Reuben Levy, who disappeared mysteriously from his house last night. His line of reasoning is: We've lost a middle-aged gentleman without any clothes on in Park Lane; we've found a middle-aged gentleman without any clothes on in Battersea. Therefore they're one and the same person. Q.E.D., and put little Thipps in quod.'

'You're very elliptical, dear,' said the Duchess mildly. 'Why should Mr Thipps be arrested even if they are the same?'

'Sugg must arrest somebody,' said Lord Peter, 'but there is one odd little bit of evidence come out which goes a long way to support Sugg's theory, only that I know it to be no go by the evidence of my own eyes. Last night at about 9.15 a young woman was strollin' up the Battersea Park Road for purposes best known to herself, when she saw a gentleman in a fur coat and top-hat saunterin' along under an umbrella, lookin' at the names of all the streets. He looked a bit out of place, so, not bein' a shy girl, you see,

44

she walked up to him, and said: 'Good-evening.' 'Can you tell me, please,' says the mysterious stranger, 'whether this street leads into Prince of Wales Road?' She said it did, and further asked him in a jocular manner what he was doing with himself and all the rest of it, only she wasn't altogether so explicit about that part of the conversation, because she was unburdenin' her heart to Sugg, d'you see, and he's paid by a grateful country to have very pure, high-minded ideals, what? Anyway, the old boy said he couldn't attend to her just then as he had an appointment. 'I've got to go and see a man, my dear,' was how she said he put it, and he walked on up Alexandra Avenue toward Prince of Wales Road. She was starin' after him, still rather surprised, when she was joined by a friend of hers, who said: 'It's no good wasting your time with him — that's Levy — I knew him when I lived in the West End, and the girls used to call him Seagreen Incorruptible' — friend's name suppressed, owing to implications of story, but girl vouches for what was said. She thought no more about it till the milkman brought news this morning of the excitement at Queen Caroline Mansions; then she went round, though not likin' the police as a rule, and asked the man there whether the dead gentleman had a beard and glasses. Told he had glasses but no beard, she incautiously said: 'Oh, then, it isn't him,' and the man said: 'Isn't who?' and collared her. That's her story. Sugg's delighted, of course, and quodded Thipps on the strength of it.'

'Dear me,' said the Duchess. 'I hope the poor

girl won't get into trouble.'

'Shouldn't think so,' said Lord Peter. 'Thipps is the one that's going to get it in the neck. Besides, he's done a silly thing. I got that out of Sugg, too, though he was sittin' tight on the information. Seems Thipps got into a confusion about the train he took back from Manchester. Said first he got home at 10.30. Then they pumped Gladys Horrocks, who let out he wasn't back till after 11.45. Then Thipps, bein' asked to explain the discrepancy, stammers and bungles and says, first, that he missed the train. Then Sugg makes inquiries at St Pancras and discovers that he left a bag in the cloakroom there at ten. Thipps, again asked to explain, stammers worse an' says he walked about for a few hours — met a friend — can't say who — didn't meet a friend — can't say what he did with his time — can't explain why he didn't go back for his bag — can't say what time he *did* get in — can't explain how he got a bruise on his forehead. In fact, can't explain himself at all. Gladys Horrocks interrogated again. Says, this time, Thipps came in at 10.30. Then admits she didn't hear him come in. Can't say why she didn't hear him come in. Can't say why she said first of all she *did* hear him. Bursts into tears. Contradicts herself. Everybody's suspicion roused. Quod 'em both.'

'As you put it, dear,' said the Duchess, 'it all sounds very confusing, and not quite respectable. Poor little Mr Thipps would be terribly upset by anything that wasn't respectable.'

'I wonder what he did with himself,' said Lord

Peter thoughtfully. 'I really don't think he was committing a murder. Besides, I believe the fellow had been dead a day or two, though it don't do to build too much on doctor's evidence. It's an entertainin' little problem.'

'Very curious, dear. But so sad about poor Sir Reuben. I must write a few lines to Lady Levy; I used to know her quite well, you know, dear, down in Hampshire, when she was a girl. Christine Ford, she was then, and I remember so well the dreadful trouble there was about her marrying a Jew. That was before he made his money, of course, in that oil business out in America. The family wanted her to marry Julian Freke, who did so well afterwards and was connected with the family, but she fell in love with this Mr Levy and eloped with him. He was very handsome, then, you know, dear, in a foreign-looking way, but he hadn't any means, and the Fords didn't like his religion. Of course we're all Jews nowadays, and they wouldn't have minded so much if he'd pretended to be something else, like that Mr Simons we met at Mrs Porchester's, who always tells everybody that he got his nose in Italy at the Renaissance, and claims to be descended somehow or other from La Bella Simonetta — so foolish, you know, dear — as if anybody believed it; and I'm sure some Jews are very good people, and personally I'd much rather they believed something, though of course it must be very inconvenient, what with not working on Saturdays and circumcising the poor little babies and everything depending on the new moon and that funny kind of meat they

47

have with such a slang-sounding name, and never being able to have bacon for breakfast. Still, there it was, and it was much better for the girl to marry him if she was really fond of him, though I believe young Freke was really devoted to her, and they're still great friends. Not that there was ever a real engagement, only a sort of understanding with her father, but he's never married, you know, and lives all by himself in that big house next to the hospital, though he's very rich and distinguished now, and I know ever so many people have tried to get hold of him — there was Lady Mainwaring wanted him for that eldest girl of hers, though I remember saying at the time it was no use expecting a surgeon to be taken in by a figure that was all padding — they have so many opportunities of judging, you know, dear.'

'Lady Levy seems to have had the knack of makin' people devoted to her,' said Peter. 'Look at the sea green incorruptible Levy.'

'That's quite true, dear; she was a most delightful girl, and they say her daughter is just like her. I rather lost sight of them when she married, and you know your father didn't care much about business people, but I knew everybody always said they were a model couple. In fact it was a proverb that Sir Reuben was as well loved at home as he was hated abroad. I don't mean in foreign countries, you know, dear — just the proverbial way of putting things — like 'a saint abroad and a devil at home' — only the other way on, reminding one of the *Pilgrim's Progress*.'

'Yes,' said Peter, 'I daresay the old man made one or two enemies.'

'Dozens, dear — such a dreadful place, the City, isn't it? Everybody Ishmaels together — though I don't suppose Sir Reuben would like to be called that, would he? Doesn't it mean illegitimate, or not a proper Jew, anyway? I always did get confused with those Old Testament characters.'

Lord Peter laughed and yawned.

'I think I'll turn in for an hour or two,' he said. 'I must be back in town at eight — Parker's coming to breakfast.'

The Duchess looked at the clock, which marked five minutes to three.

'I'll send up your breakfast at half-past six, dear,' she said. 'I hope you'll find everything all right. I told them just to slip a hot-water bottle in; those linen sheets are so chilly; you can put it out if it's in your way.'

4

' — So there it is, Parker,' said Lord Peter, pushing his coffee-cup aside and lighting his after-breakfast pipe; 'you may find it leads you to something, though it don't seem to get me any further with my bathroom problem. Did you do anything more at that after I left?'

'No; but I've been on the roof this morning.'

'The deuce you have — what an energetic devil you are! I say, Parker, I think this co-operative scheme is an uncommonly good one. It's much easier to work on someone else's job than one's own — gives one that delightful feelin' of interferin' and bossin' about, combined with the glorious sensation that another fellow is takin' all one's own work off one's hands. You scratch my back and I'll scratch yours, what? Did you find anything?'

'Not very much. I looked for any footmarks of course, but naturally, with all this rain, there wasn't a sign. Of course, if this were a detective story, there'd have been a convenient shower exactly an hour before the crime and a beautiful set of marks which could only have come there between two and three in the morning, but this being real life in a London November, you might as well expect footprints in Niagara. I searched the roofs right along — and came to the jolly conclusion that any person in any blessed flat in the blessed row might have done it. All the staircases open on to the roof and the leads are quite flat; you can walk along as easy as along Shaftesbury Avenue. Still, I've got some evidence that the body did walk along there.'

'What's that?'

Parker brought out his pocket-book and extracted a few shreds of material, which he laid before his friend.

'One was caught in the gutter just above Thipps's bathroom window, another in a crack of the stone parapet just over it, and the rest came from the chimney-stack behind, where they had caught in an iron stanchion. What do you make of them?'

Lord Peter scrutinised them very carefully through his lens.

'Interesting,' he said, 'damned interesting. Have you developed those plates, Bunter?' he added, as that discreet assistant came in with the post.

'Yes, my lord.'

'Caught anything?'

'I don't know whether to call it anything or not, my lord,' said Bunter, dubiously. 'I'll bring the prints in.'

'Do,' said Wimsey. 'Hallo! here's our advertisement about the gold chain in *The Times* — very nice it looks: 'Write, phone or call 110A Piccadilly.' Perhaps it would have been safer to put a box number, though I always think that the franker you are with people, the more you're likely to deceive 'em; so unused is the modern world to the open hand and the guileless heart, what?'

'But you don't think the fellow who left that chain on the body is going to give himself away by coming here and inquiring about it?'

'I don't, fathead,' said Lord Peter, with the easy politeness of the real aristocracy, 'that's why I've tried to get hold of the jeweller who originally sold the chain. See?' He pointed to the paragraph. 'It's not an old chain — hardly worn at all. Oh, thanks, Bunter. Now, see here, Parker, these are the finger-marks you noticed yesterday on the window-sash and on the far edge of the bath. I'd overlooked them; I give you full credit for the discovery. I crawl, I grovel, my name is Watson, and you need not say what you were just going to say, because I admit it all. Now we shall — Hullo, hullo, hullo!'

The three men stared at the photographs.

'The criminal,' said Lord Peter, bitterly, 'climbed over the roofs in the wet and not unnaturally got soot on his fingers. He arranged the body in the bath, and wiped away all traces of himself except two, which he obligingly left to show us how to do our job. We learn from a smudge on the floor that he wore India rubber boots, and from this admirable set of finger-prints on the edge of the bath that he had the usual number of fingers and wore rubber gloves. That's the kind of man he is. Take the fool away, gentlemen.'

He put the prints aside, and returned to an examination of the shreds of material in his hand. Suddenly he whistled softly.

'Do you make anything of these, Parker?'

'They seemed to me to be ravellings of some

coarse cotton stuff — a sheet, perhaps, or an improvised rope.'

'Yes,' said Lord Peter — 'yes. It may be a mistake — it may be *our* mistake. I wonder. Tell me, d'you think these tiny threads are long enough and strong enough to hang a man?'

He was silent, his long eyes narrowing into slits behind the smoke of his pipe.

'What do you suggest doing this morning?' asked Parker.

'Well,' said Lord Peter, 'it seems to me it's about time I took a hand in your job. Let's go round to Park Lane and see what larks Sir Reuben Levy was up to in bed last night.'

★   ★   ★

'And now, Mrs Pemming, if you would be so kind as to give me a blanket,' said Mr Bunter, coming down into the kitchen, 'and permit of me hanging a sheet across the lower part of this window, and drawing the screen across here, so — so as to shut off any reflections, if you understand me, we'll get to work.'

Sir Reuben Levy's cook, with her eyes upon Mr Bunter's gentlemanly and well-tailored appearance, hastened to produce what was necessary. Her visitor placed on the table a basket, containing a water-bottle, a silver-backed hair-brush, a pair of boots, a small roll of linoleum, and the *Letters of a Self-made Merchant to His Son*, bound in polished morocco. He drew an umbrella from beneath his arm and added it to the collection. He then advanced a ponderous photographic machine and set it up in the neighbourhood of the kitchen range; then, spreading a newspaper over the fair, scrubbed surface of the table, he began to roll up his sleeves and insinuate himself into a pair of surgical gloves. Sir Reuben Levy's valet, entering at the moment and finding him thus engaged, put aside the kitchen-maid, who was staring from a front-row position, and inspected the apparatus critically. Mr Bunter nodded brightly to him, and uncorked a small bottle of grey powder.

'Odd sort of fish, your employer, isn't he?' said the valet, carelessly.

'Very singular, indeed,' said Mr Bunter. 'Now, my dear,' he added, ingratiatingly, to the parlour maid, 'I wonder if you'd just pour a little of this grey powder over the edge of the bottle while I'm holding it — and the same with this boot — here, at the top — thank you, Miss — what is your name? Price? Oh, but you've got another name besides Price, haven't you? Mabel, eh? That's a name I'm uncommonly partial to — that's very nicely done, you've a steady hand, Miss Mabel — see that? That's the finger-marks — three there, and two here, and smudged over in both places. No, don't you touch 'em, my dear, or you'll rub the bloom off. We'll stand 'em up here till they're ready to have their portraits taken. Now then, let's take the hair-brush next. Perhaps, Mrs Pemming, you'd like to lift him up very carefully by the bristles.'

'By the bristles, Mr Bunter?'

'If you please, Mrs Pemming — and lay him

here. Now, Miss Mabel, another little exhibition of your skill, *if* you please. No — we'll try lamp-black this time. Perfect. Couldn't have done it better myself. Ah! there's a beautiful set. No smudges this time. That'll interest his lordship. Now the little book — no, I'll pick that up myself — with these gloves, you see, and by the edges — I'm a careful criminal, Mrs Pemming, I don't want to leave any traces. Dust the cover all over, Miss Mabel; now this side — that's the way to do it. Lots of prints and no smudges. All according to plan. Oh, please, Mr Graves, you mustn't touch it — it's as much as my place is worth to have it touched.'

'D'you have to do much of this sort of thing?' inquired Mr Graves, from a superior standpoint.

'Any amount,' replied Mr Bunter, with a groan calculated to appeal to Mr Graves's heart and unlock his confidence. 'If you'd kindly hold one end of this bit of linoleum, Mrs Pemming, I'll hold up this end while Miss Mabel operates. Yes, Mr Graves, it's a hard life, valeting by day and developing by night — morning tea at any time from 6.30 to 11, and criminal investigation at all hours. It's wonderful, the ideas these rich men with nothing to do get into their heads.'

'I wonder you stand it,' said Mr Graves. 'Now there's none of that here. A quiet, orderly, domestic life, Mr Bunter, has much to be said for it. Meals at regular hours; decent, respectable families to dinner — none of your painted women — and no valeting at night, there's *much* to be said for it. I don't hold with Hebrews as a rule, Mr Bunter, and of course I understand that

55

you may find it to your advantage to be in a titled family, but there's less thought of that these days, and I will say, for a self-made man, no one could call Sir Reuben vulgar, and my lady at any rate is county — Miss Ford, she was, one of the Hampshire Fords, and both of them always most considerate.'

'I agree with you, Mr Graves — his lordship and me have never held with being narrow-minded — why, yes, my dear, of course it's a foot-mark, this is the washstand linoleum. A good Jew can be a good man, that's what I've always said. And regular hours and considerate habits have a great deal to recommend them. Very simple in his tastes, now, Sir Reuben, isn't he? for such a rich man, I mean.'

'Very simple indeed,' said the cook, 'the meals he and her ladyship have when they're by themselves with Miss Rachel — well, there now — if it wasn't for the dinners, which is always good when there's company, I'd be wastin' my talents and education here, if you understand me, Mr Bunter.'

Mr Bunter added the handle of the umbrella to his collection, and began to pin a sheet across the window, aided by the house-maid.

'Admirable,' said he. 'Now, if I might have this blanket on the table and another on a towel-horse or something of that kind by way of a background — you're very kind, Mrs Pemming . . . Ah! I wish his lordship never wanted valeting at night. Many's the time I've sat up till three and four, and up again to call him early to go off Sherlocking at the other end of the country.

56

And the mud he gets on his clothes and his boots!'

'I'm sure it's a shame, Mr Bunter,' said Mrs Pemming, warmly. 'Low, I calls it. In my opinion, police-work ain't no fit occupation for a gentleman, let alone a lordship.'

'Everything made so difficult, too,' said Mr Bunter, nobly sacrificing his employer's character and his own feelings in a good cause; 'boots chucked into a corner, clothes hung up on the floor, as they say — '

'That's often the case with these men as are born with a silver spoon in their mouths,' said Mr Graves. 'Now, Sir Reuben, he's never lost his good, old-fashioned habits. Clothes folded up neat, boots put out in his dressing-room, so as a man could get them in the morning, everything made easy.'

'He forgot them the night before last, though.'

'The clothes, not the boots. Always thoughtful for others, is Sir Reuben. Ah! I hope nothing's happened to him.'

'Indeed, no, poor gentleman,' chimed in the cook, 'and as for what they're sayin', that he'd 'ave gone out surrepshous-like to do something he didn't ought, well, I'd never believe it of him, Mr Bunter, not if I was to take my dying oath upon it.'

'Ah!' said Mr Bunter, adjusting his arc-lamps and connecting them with the nearest electric light, 'and that's more than most of us could say of them as pays us.'

★ ★ ★

'Five-foot-ten,' said Lord Peter, 'and not an inch more.' He peered dubiously at the depression in the bed-clothes, and measured it a second time with the gentleman scout's vade mecum. Parker entered this particular in a neat pocket-book.

'I suppose,' he said, 'a six-foot-two man *might* leave a five-foot-ten depression if he curled himself up.'

'Have you any Scotch blood in you, Parker?' inquired his colleague, bitterly.

'Not that I know of,' replied Parker. 'Why?'

'Because of all the cautious, ungenerous, deliberate and cold-blooded devils I know,' said Lord Peter, 'you are the most cautious, ungenerous, deliberate and cold-blooded. Here am I, sweating my brains out to introduce a really sensational incident into your dull and disreputable little police investigation, and you refuse to show a single spark of enthusiasm.'

'Well, it's no good jumping at conclusions.'

'Jump? You don't even crawl distantly within sight of a conclusion. I believe if you caught the cat with her head in the cream-jug you'd say it was conceivable that the jug was empty when she got there.'

'Well, it would be conceivable, wouldn't it?'

'Curse you,' said Lord Peter. He screwed his monocle into his eye, and bent over the pillow, breathing hard and tightly through his nose. 'Here, give me the tweezers,' he said presently; 'good heavens, man, don't blow like that, you might be a whale.' He nipped up an almost invisible object from the linen.

'What is it?' asked Parker.

58

'It's a hair,' said Wimsey grimly, his hard eyes growing harder. 'Let's go and look at Levy's hats, shall we? And you might just ring for that fellow with the churchyard name, do you mind?'

Mr Graves, when summoned, found Lord Peter Wimsey squatting on the floor of the dressing-room before a row of hats arranged upside down before him.

'Here you are,' said that nobleman cheerfully. 'Now, Graves, this is a guessin' competition — a sort of three-hat trick, to mix metaphors. Here are nine hats, including three top-hats. Do you identify all these hats as belonging to Sir Reuben Levy? You do? Very good. Now I have three guesses as to which hat he wore the night he disappeared, and if I guess right, I win; if I don't, you win. See? Ready? Go. I suppose you know the answer yourself, by the way?'

'Do I understand your lordship to be asking which hat Sir Reuben wore when he went out on Monday night, your lordship?'

'No, you don't understand a bit,' said Lord Peter. 'I'm asking if *you* know — don't tell me, I'm going to guess.'

'I do know, your lordship,' said Mr Graves, reprovingly.

'Well,' said Lord Peter, 'as he was dinin' at the Ritz he wore a topper. Here are three toppers. In three guesses I'd be bound to hit the right one wouldn't I? That don't seem very sportin'. I'll take one guess. It was this one.'

He indicated the hat next the window.

'Am I right, Graves — have I got the prize?'

'That *is* the hat in question, my lord,' said Mr

59

Graves, without excitement.

'Thanks,' said Lord Peter, 'that's all I wanted to know. Ask Bunter to step up, would you?'

Mr Bunter stepped up with an aggrieved air, and his usually smooth hair ruffled by the focusing cloth.

'Oh, there you are, Bunter,' said Lord Peter; 'look here — '

'Here I am, my lord,' said Mr Bunter, with respectful reproach, 'but if you'll excuse me saying so, downstairs is where I ought to be, with all those young women about — they'll be fingering the evidence, my lord.'

'I cry you mercy,' said Lord Peter, 'but I've quarrelled hopelessly with Mr Parker and distracted the estimable Graves, and I want you to tell me what finger-prints you have found. I shan't be happy till I get it, so don't be harsh with me, Bunter.'

'Well, my lord, your lordship understands I haven't photographed them yet, but I won't deny that their appearance is interesting, my lord. The little book off the night table, my lord, has only the marks of one set of fingers — there's a little scar on the right thumb which makes them easy recognised. The hair-brush, too, my lord, has only the same set of marks. The umbrella, the toothglass and the boots all have two sets: the hand with the scarred thumb, which I take to be Sir Reuben's, my lord, and a set of smudges superimposed upon them, if I may put it that way, my lord, which may or may not be the same hand in rubber gloves. I could tell you better when I've got the photographs made, to measure them, my lord. The linoleum in front of the washstand is very gratifying indeed, my lord, if you will excuse my mentioning it. Besides the marks of Sir Reuben's boots which your lordship pointed out, there's the print of a man's naked foot — a much smaller one, my lord, not much more than a ten-inch sock, I should say if you asked me.'

Lord Peter's face became irradiated with almost a dim, religious light.

'A mistake,' he breathed, 'a mistake, a little one, but he can't afford it. When was the linoleum washed last, Bunter?'

'Monday morning, my lord. The housemaid did it and remembered to mention it. Only remark she's made yet, and it's to the point. The other domestics — '

His features expressed disdain.

'What did I say, Parker? Five-foot-ten and not an inch longer. And he didn't dare to use the hair-brush. Beautiful. But he *had* to risk the top-hat. Gentleman can't walk home in the rain late at night without a hat, you know, Parker. Look! what do you make of it? Two sets of finger-prints on everything but the book and the brush, two sets of feet on the linoleum, and two kinds of hair in the hat!'

He lifted the top-hat to the light, and extracted the evidence with tweezers.

'Think of it, Parker — to remember the hair-brush and forget the hat — to remember his fingers all the time, and to make that one careless step on the tell-tale linoleum. Here they are, you see, black hair and tan hair — black hair

61

in the bowler and the panama, and black and tan in last night's topper. And then, just to make certain that we're on the right track, just one little auburn hair on the pillow, on this pillow, Parker, which isn't quite in the right place. It almost brings tears to my eyes.'

'Do you mean to say — ?' said the detective, slowly.

'I mean to say,' said Lord Peter, 'that it was not Sir Reuben Levy whom the cook saw last night on the doorstep. I say that it was another man, perhaps a couple of inches shorter, who came here in Levy's clothes and let himself in with Levy's latchkey. Oh, he was a bold, cunning devil, Parker. He had on Levy's boots, and every stitch of Levy's clothing down to the skin. He had rubber gloves on his hands which he never took off, and he did everything he could to make us think that Levy slept here last night. He took his chances, and won. He walked upstairs, he undressed, he even washed and cleaned his teeth, though he didn't use the hair-brush for fear of leaving red hairs in it. He had to guess what Levy did with boots and clothes; one guess was wrong and the other right, as it happened. The bed must look as if it had been slept in, so he gets in, and lies there in his victim's very pyjamas. Then, in the morning sometime, probably in the deadest hour between two and three, he gets up, dresses himself in his own clothes that he has brought with him in a bag, and creeps downstairs. If anybody wakes, he is lost, but he is a bold man, and he takes his chance. He knows that people do not wake as a rule — and they don't wake. He opens the street door which he left on the latch when he came in — he listens for the stray passer-by or the policeman on his beat. He slips out. He pulls the door quietly to with the latchkey. He walks briskly away in rubber-soled shoes — he's the kind of criminal who isn't complete without rubber-soled shoes. In a few minutes he is at Hyde Park Corner. After that — '

He paused and added:

'He did all that, and unless he had nothing at stake, he had everything at stake. Either Sir Reuben Levy had been spirited away for some silly practical joke, or the man with the auburn hair has the guilt of murder upon his soul.'

'Dear me!' ejaculated the detective, 'you're very dramatic about it.'

Lord Peter passed his hand rather wearily over his hair.

'My true friend,' he murmured in a voice supercharged with emotion, 'you recall me to the nursery rhymes of my youth — the sacred duty of flippancy:

There was an old man of Whitehaven
Who danced a quadrille with a raven,
But they said: 'It's absurd
To encourage that bird' —
So they smashed that old man of White-
haven.

That's the correct attitude, Parker. Here's a poor old buffer spirited away — such a joke — and I don't believe he'd hurt a fly himself — that

63

makes it funnier. D'you know, Parker, I don't care frightfully about this case after all.'

'Which, this or yours?'

'Both. I say, Peter, shall we go quietly home and have lunch and go to the Coliseum?'

'You can if you like,' replied the detective; 'but you forget I do this for my bread and butter.'

'And I haven't even that excuse,' said Lord Peter; 'well, what's the next move? What would you do in my case?'

'I'd do some good, hard grind,' said Parker. 'I'd distrust every bit of work Sugg ever did, and I'd get the family history of every tenant of every flat in Queen Caroline Mansions. I'd examine all their box-rooms and roof-traps, and I would inveigle them into conversations and suddenly bring in the words 'body' and 'pince-nez', and see if they wriggled, like those modern psycho-what's-his-names.'

'You would, would you?' said Lord Peter with a grin. 'Well, we've exchanged cases, you know, so just you toddle off and do it. I'm going to have a jolly time at Wyndham's.'

Parker made a grimace.

'Well,' he said. 'I don't suppose you'd ever do it, so I'd better. You'll never become a professional till you learn to do a little work, Wimsey. How about lunch?'

'I'm invited out,' said Lord Peter, magnificently. 'I'll run round and change at the club. Can't feed with Freddy Arbuthnot in these bags; Bunter!'

'Yes, my lord.'

'Pack up if you're ready, and come round and

64

wash my face and hands for me at the club.'

'Work here for another two hours, my lord. Can't do with less than thirty minutes' exposure. The current's none too strong.'

'You see how I'm bullied by my own man, Parker? Well, I must bear it, I suppose. Ta-ta!'

He whistled his way downstairs.

The conscientious Mr Parker, with a groan, settled down to a systematic search through Sir Reuben Levy's papers, with the assistance of a plate of ham sandwiches and a bottle of Bass.

★   ★   ★

Lord Peter and the Honourable Freddy Arbuthnot, looking together like an advertisement for gents' trouserings strolled into the dining-room at Wyndham's.

'Haven't seen you for an age,' said the Honourable Freddy, 'what have you been doin' with yourself?'

'Oh, foolin' about,' said Lord Peter, languidly.

'Thick or clear, sir?' inquired the waiter of the Honourable Freddy.

'Which'll you have, Wimsey?' said that gentleman, transferring the burden of selection to his guest, 'they're both equally poisonous.'

'Well, clear's less trouble to lick out of the spoon,' said Lord Peter.

'Clear,' said the Honourable Freddy.

'Consommé Polonais,' agreed the waiter. 'Very nice, sir.'

Conversation languished until the Honourable Freddy found a bone in the filleted sole, and sent for the head waiter to explain its presence. When this matter had been adjusted Lord Peter found energy to say:

'Sorry to hear about your guv'nor, old man.'

'Yes, poor old buffer,' said the Honourable Freddy; 'they say he can't last long now. What? Oh! the Montrachet '08. There's nothing fit to drink in this place,' he added gloomily.

After this deliberate insult to a noble vintage there was a further pause, till Lord Peter said: 'How's 'Change?'

'Rotten,' said the Honourable Freddy.

He helped himself gloomily to *salmis* of game.

'Can I do anything?' asked Lord Peter.

'Oh, no, thanks — very decent of you, but it'll pan out all right in time.'

'This isn't bad *salmis*,' said Lord Peter.

'I've eaten worse,' admitted his friend.

'What about those Argentines?' inquired Lord Peter. 'Here, waiter, there's a bit of cork in my glass.'

'Cork?' cried the Honourable Freddy, with something approaching animation; 'you'll hear about this, waiter. It's an amazing thing a fellow who's paid to do the job can't manage to take a cork out of a bottle. What you say? Argentines? Gone all to hell. Old Levy bunkin' off like that's knocked the bottom out of the market.'

'You don't say so,' said Lord Peter; 'what d'you suppose has happened to the old man?'

'Cursed if I know,' said the Honourable Freddy; 'knocked on the head by the bears, I should think.'

'P'r'aps he's gone off on his own,' suggested

66

Lord Peter. 'Double life, you know. Giddy old blighters, some of these City men.'

'Oh, no,' said the Honourable Freddy, faintly roused; 'no, hang it all, Wimsey, I wouldn't care to say that. He's a decent old domestic bird, and his daughter's a charmin' girl. Besides, he's straight enough — he'd *do* you down fast enough, but he wouldn't *let* you down. Old Anderson is badly cut up about it.'

'Who's Anderson?'

'Chap with property out there. He belongs here. He was goin' to meet Levy on Tuesday. He's afraid those railway people will get in now, and then it'll be all U.P.'

'Who's runnin' the railway people over here?' inquired Lord Peter.

'Yankee blighter, John P. Milligan. He's got an option, or says he has. You can't trust these brutes.'

'Can't Anderson hold on?'

'Anderson isn't Levy. Hasn't got the shekels. Besides, he's only one. Levy covers the ground — he could boycott Milligan's beastly railway if he liked. That's where he's got the pull, you see.'

'B'lieve I met the Milligan man somewhere,' said Lord Peter, thoughtfully; 'ain't he a hulking brute with black hair and a beard?'

'You're thinkin' of somebody else,' said the Honourable Freddy. 'Milligan don't stand any higher than I do, unless you call five-feet-ten hulking — and he's bald, anyway.'

Lord Peter considered this over the Gorgonzola. Then he said:

'Didn't know Levy had a charmin' daughter.'

'Oh, yes,' said the Honourable Freddy, with an elaborate detachment. 'Met her and Mamma last year abroad. That's how I got to know the old man. He's been very decent. Let me into this Argentine business on the ground floor, don't you know?'

'Well,' said Lord Peter, 'you might do worse. Money's money, ain't it? And Lady Levy is quite a redeemin' point, At least, my mother knew her people.'

'Oh, *she's* all right,' said the Honourable Freddy, 'and the old man's nothing to be ashamed of nowadays. He's self-made, of course, but he don't pretend to be anything else. No side. Toddles off to business on a 96 bus every morning. 'Can't make up my mind to taxis, my boy,' he says. 'I had to look at every halfpenny when I was a young man, and I can't get out of the way of it now.' Though, if he's takin' his family out, nothing's too good. Rachel — that's the girl — always laughs at the old man's little economies.'

'I suppose they've sent for Lady Levy,' said Lord Peter.

'I suppose so,' agreed the other. 'I'd better pop round and express sympathy or somethin', what? Wouldn't look well not to, d'you think? But it's deuced awkward. What am I to say?'

'I don't think it matters much what you say,' said Lord Peter helpfully. 'I should ask if you can do anything.'

'Thanks,' said the lover, 'I will. Energetic young man. Count on me. Always at your service. Ring me up any time of the day or night.

That's the line to take, don't you think?'
'That's the idea,' said Lord Peter.

★ ★ ★

Mr John P. Milligan, the London representative of the great Milligan railroad and shipping company, was dictating code cables to his secretary in an office in Lombard Street, when a card was brought up to him, bearing the simple legend:

LORD PETER WIMSEY
Marlborough Club

Mr Milligan was annoyed at the interruption, but, like many of his nation, if he had a weak point, it was the British aristocracy. He postponed for a few minutes the elimination from the map of a modest but promising farm, and directed that the visitor should be shown up.

'Good-afternoon,' said the nobleman, ambling genially in, 'it's most uncommonly good of you to let me come round wastin' your time like this. I'll try not to be too long about it, though I'm not awfully good at comin' to the point. My brother never would let me stand for the county, y'know — said I wandered on so nobody'd know what I was talkin' about.'

'Pleased to meet you, Lord Wimsey,' said Mr Milligan. 'Won't you take a seat?'

'Thanks,' said Lord Peter, 'but I'm not a peer, you know — that's my brother Denver. My name's Peter. It's a silly name, I always think, so old-world and full of homely virtue and that sort of thing, but my godfathers and godmothers in my baptism are responsible for that, I suppose, officially — which is rather hard on them, you know, as they didn't actually choose it. But we always have a Peter, after the third duke, who betrayed five kings somewhere about the Wars of the Roses, though come to think of it, it ain't anything to be proud of. Still, one has to make the best of it.'

Mr Milligan, thus ingeniously placed at that disadvantage which attends ignorance, manoeuvred for position, and offered his interrupter a Corona Corona.

'Thanks, awfully,' said Lord Peter, 'though you really mustn't tempt me to stay here burblin' all afternoon. By Jove, Mr Milligan, if you offer people such comfortable chairs and cigars like these, I wonder they don't come an' live in your office.' He added mentally: 'I wish to goodness I could get those long-toed boots off you. How's a man to know the size of your feet? And a head like a potato. It's enough to make one swear.'

'Say now, Lord Peter,' said Mr Milligan, 'can I do anything for you?'

'Well, d'you know,' said Lord Peter, 'I'm wonderin' if you would. It's damned cheek to ask you, but fact is, it's my mother, you know. Wonderful woman, but don't realise what it means, demands on the time of a busy man like you. We don't understand hustle over here, you know, Mr Milligan.'

'Now don't you mention that,' said Mr Milligan; 'I'd be surely charmed to do anything to oblige the Duchess.'

He felt a momentary qualm as to whether a duke's mother were also a duchess, but breathed more freely as Lord Peter went on:

'Thanks — that's uncommonly good of you. Well, now, it's like this. My mother — most energetic, self-sacrificin' woman, don't you see, is thinkin' of gettin' up a sort of a charity bazaar down at Denver this winter, in aid of the church roof, y'know. Very sad case, Mr Milligan — fine old antique — early English windows and decorated angel roof, and all that — all tumblin' to pieces, rain pourin' in and so on — vicar catchin' rheumatism at early service, owin' to the draught blowin' in over the altar — you know the sort of thing. They've got a man down startin' on it — little beggar called Thipps — lives with an aged mother in Battersea — vulgar little beast, but quite good on angel roofs and things, I'm told.'

At this point, Lord Peter watched his interlocutor narrowly, but finding that this rigmarole produced in him no reaction more startling than polite interest tinged with faint bewilderment, he abandoned this line of investigation and proceeded:

'I say, I beg your pardon, frightfully — I'm afraid I'm bein' beastly long-winded. Fact is, my mother is gettin' up this bazaar, and she thought it'd be an awfully interestin' side-show to have some lectures — sort of little talks, y'know — by eminent business men of all nations. 'How I did it' kind of touch, y'know — 'A Drop of Oil with a Kerosene King' — 'Cash Conscience and

71

Cocoa' and so on. It would interest people down there no end. You see, all my mother's friends will be there, and we've none of us any money — not what you'd call money, I mean — I expect our incomes wouldn't pay your telephone calls, would they? — but we like awfully to hear about the people who can make money. Gives us a sort of uplifted feelin', don't you know. Well, anyway, I mean, my mother'd be frightfully pleased and grateful to you, Mr Milligan, if you'd come down and give us a few words as a representative American. It needn't take more than ten minutes or so, y'know, because the local people can't understand much beyond shootin' and huntin', and my mother's crowd can't keep their minds on anythin' more than ten minutes together, but we'd really appreciate it very much if you'd come and stay a day or two and just give us a little breezy word on the almighty dollar.'

'Why, yes,' said Mr Milligan, 'I'd like to, Lord Peter. It's kind of the Duchess to suggest it. It's a very sad thing when these fine old antiques begin to wear out. I'll come with great pleasure. And perhaps you'd be kind enough to accept a little donation to the Restoration Fund.'

This unexpected development nearly brought Lord Peter up all standing. To pump, by means of an ingenious lie, a hospitable gentleman whom you are inclined to suspect of a peculiarly malicious murder, and to accept from him in the course of the proceedings a large cheque for a charitable object, has something about it unpalatable to any but the hardened Secret Service Agent. Lord Peter temporised.

72

'That's awfully decent of you,' he said. 'I'm sure they'd be no end grateful. But you'd better not give it to me, you know, I might spend it, or lose it. I'm not very reliable, I'm afraid. The vicar's the right person — the Rev. Constantine Throgmorton, St John-before-the-Latin-Gate Vicarage, Duke's Denver, if you like to send it there.'

'I will,' said Mr Milligan. 'Will you write it out now for a thousand pounds, Scoot, in case it slips my mind later?'

The secretary, a sandy-haired young man with a long chin and no eyebrows, silently did as he was requested. Lord Peter looked from the bald head of Mr Milligan to the red head of the secretary, hardened his heart and tried again.

'Well, I'm no end grateful to you, Mr Milligan, and so'll my mother be when I tell her. I'll let you know the date of the bazaar — it's not quite settled yet, and I've got to see some other businessmen, don't you know. I thought of askin' someone from the big newspaper combines to represent British advertisin' talent, what? — and a friend of mine promises me a leadin' German financier — very interestin' if there ain't too much feelin' against it down in the country, and I'll have to find somebody or other to do the Hebrew point of view. I thought of askin' Levy, y'know, only he's floated off in this inconvenient way.'

'Yes,' said Milligan, 'that's a very curious thing, though I don't mind saying, Lord Peter, that it's a convenience to me. He had a cinch on my railroad combine, but I'd nothing against

73

him personally, and if he turns up after I've brought off a little deal I've got on, I'll be happy to give him the right hand of welcome.'

A vision passed through Lord Peter's mind of Sir Reuben kept somewhere in custody till a financial crisis was over. This was exceedingly possible, and far more agreeable than his earlier conjecture; it also agreed better with the impression he was forming of Mr Milligan.

'Well, it's a rum go,' said Lord Peter, 'but I daresay he had his reason. Much better not inquire into people's reasons, y'know, what? Specially as a police friend of mine who's connected with the case says the old johnnie dyed his hair before he went.'

Out of the tail of his eye, Lord Peter saw the red-headed secretary add up five columns of figures simultaneously and jot down the answer.

'Dyed his hair, did he?' said Mr Milligan.

'Dyed it red,' said Lord Peter. The secretary looked up. 'Odd thing is,' continued Wimsey, 'they can't lay hands on the bottle. Somethin' fishy there, don't you think, what?'

The secretary's interest seemed to have evaporated. He inserted a fresh sheet into his looseleaf ledger and carried forward a row of digits from the preceding page.

'I daresay there's nothin' in it,' said Lord Peter, rising to go. 'Well, it's uncommonly good of you to be bothered with me like this, Mr Milligan; my mother'll be no end pleased. She'll write you about the date.'

'I'm charmed,' said Mr Milligan, 'very pleased to have met you.'

Mr Scoot rose silently to open the door, uncoiling as he did so a portentous length of thin leg, hitherto hidden by the desk. With a mental sigh Lord Peter estimated him at six-foot-four.

'It's a pity I can't put Scoot's head on Milligan's shoulders,' said Lord Peter, emerging into the swirl of the city, 'and what *will* my mother say?'

5

Mr Parker was a bachelor, and occupied a Georgian but inconvenient flat at No. 12A Great Ormond Street, for which he paid a pound a week. His exertions in the cause of civilisation were rewarded, not by a gift of diamonds, rings from empresses or munificent cheques from grateful Prime Ministers, but by a modest, though sufficient salary, drawn from the pockets of the British taxpayer. He awoke, after a long day of arduous and inconclusive labour, to the smell of burnt porridge. Through his bedroom window, hygienically open top and bottom, a raw fog was rolling slowly in, and the sight of a pair of winter pants, flung hastily over a chair the previous night, fretted him with a sense of the sordid absurdity of the human form. The telephone bell rang, and he crawled wretchedly out of bed and into the sitting-room, where Mrs Munns, who did for him by the day, was laying the table, sneezing as she went.

Mr Bunter was speaking.

'His lordship says he'd be very glad, sir, if you could make it convenient to step round to breakfast.'

If the odour of kidneys and bacon had been wafted along the wire, Mr Parker could not have experienced a more vivid sense of consolation.

'Tell his lordship I'll be with him in half an

hour,' he said, thankfully, and plunging into the bathroom, which was also the kitchen, he informed Mrs Munns, who was just making tea from a kettle which had gone off the boil, that he should be out to breakfast.

'You can take the porridge home for the family,' he added, viciously, and flung off his dressing-gown with such determination that Mrs Munns could only scuttle away with a snort.

A 19 bus deposited him in Piccadilly only fifteen minutes later than his rather sanguine impulse had prompted him to suggest, and Mr Bunter served him with glorious food, incomparable coffee, and the *Daily Mail* before a blazing fire of wood and coal. A distant voice singing the '*et interum venturus est*' from Bach's Mass in B minor proclaimed that for the owner of the flat cleanliness and godliness met at least once a day, and presently Lord Peter roamed in, moist and verbena-scented, in a bath-robe cheerfully patterned with unnaturally variegated peacocks.

'Mornin', old dear,' said that gentleman; 'beast of a day, ain't it? Very good of you to trundle out in it, but I had a letter I wanted you to see, and I hadn't the energy to come round to your place. Bunter and I've been makin' a night of it.'

'What's the letter?' asked Parker.

'Never talk business with your mouth full,' said Lord Peter, reprovingly; 'have some Oxford marmalade — and then I'll show you my Dante; they brought it round last night. What ought I to read this morning, Bunter?'

77

'Lord Erith's collection is going to be sold, my lord. There is a column about it in the *Morning Post*. I think your lordship should look at this review of Sir Julian Freke's new book on *The Physiological Bases of the Conscience* in *The Times Literary Supplement*. Then there is a very singular little burglary in the *Chronicle*, my lord, and an attack on titled families in the *Herald* — rather ill-written, if I may say so, but not without unconscious humour which your lordship will appreciate.'

'All right, give me that and the burglary,' said his lordship.

'I have looked over the other papers,' pursued Mr Bunter, indicating a formidable pile, 'and marked your lordship's after-breakfast reading.'

'Oh, pray don't allude to it,' said Lord Peter, 'you take my appetite away.'

There was silence, but for the crunching of toast and the crackling of paper.

'I see they adjourned the inquest,' said Parker presently.

'Nothing else to do,' said Lord Peter, 'but Lady Levy arrived last night, and will have to go and fail to identify the body this morning for Sugg's benefit.'

'Time, too,' said Mr Parker shortly.

Silence fell again.

'I don't think much of your burglary, Bunter,' said Lord Peter. 'Competent, of course, but no imagination. I want imagination in a criminal. Where's the *Morning Post*?'

After a further silence, Lord Peter said: 'You might send for the catalogue. Bunter; that

Apollonios Rhodios[1] might be worth looking at. No, I'm damned if I'm going to stodge through that review, but you can stick the book on the library list if you like. His book on crime was entertainin' enough as far as it went, but the fellow's got a bee in his bonnet. Thinks God's a secretion of the liver — all right once in a way, but there's no need to keep on about it. There's nothing you can't prove if your outlook is only sufficiently limited. Look at Sugg.'

'I beg your pardon,' said Parker. 'I wasn't attending. Argentines are steadying a little, I see.'

'Milligan,' said Lord Peter.

'Oil's in a bad way. Levy's made a difference there. That funny little boom in Peruvians that came on just before he disappeared has died away again. I wonder if he was concerned in it. D'you know at all?'

'I'll find out,' said Lord Peter, 'what was it?'

'Oh, an absolutely dud enterprise that hadn't been heard of for years. It suddenly took a little lease of life last week. I happened to notice it because my mother got let in for a couple of hundred shares a long time ago. It never paid a dividend. Now it's petered out again.'

Wimsey pushed his plate aside and lit a pipe.

'Having finished, I don't mind doing some work,' he said. 'How did you get on yesterday?'

---

[1] Apollonios Rhodios. Lorenzobodi Alopa. Firenze. 1496. (4to.) The excitement attendant on the solution of the Battersea Mystery did not prevent Lord Peter from securing this rare work before his departure for Corsica.

'I didn't,' replied Parker. 'I sleuthed up and down those flats in my own bodily shape and two different disguises. I was a gas-meter man and a collector for a Home for Lost Doggies, and I didn't get a thing to go on, except a servant in the top flat at the Battersea Bridge Road end of the row who said she thought she heard a bump on the roof one night. Asked which night, she couldn't rightly say. Asked if it was Monday night, she thought it very likely. Asked if it mightn't have been that high wind on Saturday night that blew my chimney-pot off, she couldn't say but what it might have been. Asked if she was sure it was on the roof and not inside the flat, said to be sure they did find a picture tumbled down next morning. Very suggestible girl. I saw your friends, Mr and Mrs Appledore, who received me coldly, but could make no definite complaint about Thipps except that his mother dropped her h's, and that he once called on them uninvited, armed with a pamphlet about anti-vivisection. The Indian colonel on the first floor was loud, but unexpectedly friendly. He gave me Indian curry for supper and some good whisky, but he's a sort of hermit, and all *he* could tell me was that he couldn't stand Mrs Appledore.'

'Did you get nothing at the house?'

'Only Levy's private diary. I brought it away with me. Here it is. It doesn't tell one much, though. It's full of entries like: 'Tom and Annie to dinner'; and 'My dear wife's birthday; gave her an old opal ring'; 'Mr Arbuthnot dropped in to tea; he wants to marry Rachel, but I should

80

like someone steadier for my treasure.' Still, I thought it would show who came to the house and so on. He evidently wrote it up at night. There's no entry for Monday.'

'I expect it'll be useful,' said Lord Peter, turning over the pages. 'Poor old buffer. I say, I'm not so certain now he was done away with.'

He detailed to Mr Parker his day's work.

'Arbuthnot?' said Parker, 'is that the Arbuthnot of the diary?'

'I suppose so. I hunted him up because I knew he was fond of fooling round the Stock Exchange. As for Milligan, he *looks* all right, but I believe he's pretty ruthless in business and you never can tell. Then there's the red-haired secretary — lightnin' calculator man with a face like a fish, keeps on sayin' nuthin' — got the Tarbaby in his family tree, I should think. Milligan's got a jolly good motive for, at any rate, suspendin' Levy for a few days. Then there's the new man.'

'What new man?'

'Ah, that's the letter I mentioned to you. Where did I put it? — here we are. Good parchment paper, printed address of solicitor's office in Salisbury, and postmark to correspond. Very precisely written with a fine nib by an elderly business man of old-fashioned habits.'

Parker took the letter and read:

'CRIMPLESHAM AND WRIMPLESHAM,
'*Solicitors,*
'MILFORD HILL,
SALISBURY,
'17 November, 192 – .

81

'SIR,

'With reference to your advertisement today in the personal column of *The Times*, I am disposed to believe that the eyeglasses and chain in question may be those I lost on the L.B. & S.C. Electric Railway while visiting London last Monday. I left Victoria by the 5.45 train, and did not notice my loss till I arrived at Balham. This indication and the optician's specification of the glasses, which I enclose, should suffice at once as an identification and a guarantee of my *bona fides*. If the glasses should prove to be mine, I should be greatly obliged to you if you would kindly forward them to me by registered post, as the chain was a present from my daughter, and is one of my dearest possessions.

'Thanking you in advance for this kindness, and regretting the trouble to which I shall be putting you, I am,

'Yours very truly,
'THOS. CRIMPLESHAM.

'Lord Peter Wimsey,
  '110A Piccadilly, W.
'(Encl.).'

'Dear me,' said Parker, 'this is what you might call unexpected.'

'Either it is some extraordinary misunderstanding,' said Lord Peter, 'or Mr Crimplesham is a very bold and cunning villain. Or possibly, of course, they are the wrong glasses. We may as well get a ruling on that point at once. I suppose the glasses are at the Yard. I wish you'd just ring 'em up and ask 'em to send round an optician's description of them at once — and you might ask at the same time whether it's a very common prescription.'

'Right you are,' said Parker, and took the receiver off its hook.

'And now,' said his friend, when the message was delivered, 'just come into the library for a minute.'

On the library table, Lord Peter had spread out a series of bromide prints, some dry, some damp, and some but half-washed.

'These little ones are the originals of the photos we've been taking,' said Lord Peter, 'and these big ones are enlargements all made to precisely the same scale. This one here is the footmark on the linoleum; we'll put that by itself at present. Now these finger-prints can be divided into five lots. I've numbered 'em on the prints — see? — and made a list:

'A. The finger-prints of Levy himself, off his little bedside book and his hair-brush — this and this — you can't mistake the little scar on the thumb.

'B. The smudges made by the gloved fingers of the man who slept in Levy's room on Monday night. They show clearly on the water-bottle and on the boots — super-imposed on Levy's. They are very distinct on the boots — surprisingly so for gloved hands, and I deduce that the gloves were rubber ones and had recently been in water.

83

'Here's another interestin' point. Levy walked in the rain on Monday night, as we know, and these dark marks are mud-splashes. You see they lie *over* Levy's finger-prints in every case. Now see: on this left boot we find the stranger's thumb-mark *over* the mud on the leather above the heel. That's a funny place to find a thumb-mark on a boot, isn't it? That is, if Levy took off his own boots. But it's the place you'd expect to see it if somebody forcibly removed his boots for him. Again, most of the stranger's finger-marks come *over* the mud-marks, but here is one splash of mud which comes on top of them again. Which makes me infer that the stranger came back to Park Lane, wearing Levy's boots, in a cab, carriage or car, but that at some point or other he walked a little way — just enough to tread in a puddle and get a splash on the boots. What do you say?'

'Very pretty,' said Parker. 'A bit intricate, though, and the marks are not all that I could wish a finger-print to be.'

'Well, I won't lay too much stress on it. But it fits in with our previous ideas. Now let's turn to:

'C. The prints obligingly left by my own particular villain on the further edge of Thipps's bath, where you spotted them, and I ought to be scourged for not having spotted them. The left hand, you notice, the base of the palm and the fingers, but not the tips, looking as though he had steadied himself on the edge of the bath while leaning down to adjust something at the bottom, the pince-nez perhaps. Gloved, you see, but showing no ridge or seam of any kind — I

84

say rubber, you say rubber. That's that. Now see here:

'D and E come off a visiting-card of mine. There's this thing at the corner, marked F, but that you can disregard; in the original document it's a sticky mark left by the thumb of the youth who took it from me, after first removing a piece of chewing-gum from his teeth with his finger to tell me that Mr Milligan might or might not be disengaged. D and E are the thumb-marks of Mr Milligan and his red-haired secretary. I'm not clear which is which, but I saw the youth with the chewing-gum hand the card to the secretary, and when I got into the inner shrine I saw John P. Milligan standing with it in his hand, so it's one or the other, and for the moment it's immaterial to our purpose which is which. I boned the card from the table when I left.

'Well, now, Parker, here's what's been keeping Bunter and me up till the small hours. I've measured and measured every way backwards and forwards till my head's spinnin', and I've stared till I'm nearly blind, but I'm hanged if I can make my mind up. Question 1. Is C identical with B? Question 2. Is D or E identical with B? There's nothing to go on but the size and shape, of course, and the marks are so faint — what do you think?'

Parker shook his head doubtfully.

'I think E might almost be put out of the question,' he said, 'it seems such an excessively long and narrow thumb. But I think there is a decided resemblance between the span of B on the water-bottle and C on the bath. And I don't see any reason why D shouldn't be the same as B, only there's so little to judge from.'

'Your untutored judgement and my measurements have brought us both to the same conclusion — if you can call it a conclusion,' said Lord Peter, bitterly.

'Another thing,' said Parker. 'Why on earth should we try to connect B with C? The fact that you and I happen to be friends doesn't make it necessary to conclude that the two cases we happen to be interested in have any organic connection with one another. Why should they? The only person who thinks they have is Sugg, and he's nothing to go by. It would be different if there were any truth in the suggestion that the man in the bath was Levy, but we know for a certainty he wasn't. It's ridiculous to suppose that the same man was employed in committing two totally distinct crimes on the same night, one in Battersea and the other in Park Lane.'

'I know,' said Wimsey, 'though of course we mustn't forget that Levy *was* in Battersea at the time, and now we know he didn't return home at twelve as we supposed, we've no reason to think he ever left Battersea at all.'

'True. But there are other places in Battersea besides Thipps's bathroom. And he *wasn't* in Thipps's bathroom. In fact, come to think of it, that's the one place in the universe where we know definitely that he wasn't. So what's Thipps's bath got to do with it?'

'I don't know,' said Lord Peter. 'Well, perhaps we shall get something better to go on today.'

He leaned back in his chair and smoked

thoughtfully for some time over the papers which Bunter had marked for him.

'They've got you out in the limelight,' he said. 'Thank Heaven, Sugg hates me too much to give me any publicity. What a dull Agony Column! 'Darling Pipsy — Come back soon to your distracted Popsey' — and the usual young man in need of financial assistance, and the usual injunction to 'Remember thy Creator in the days of thy youth'. Hullo! there's the bell. Oh, it's our answer from Scotland Yard.'

The note from Scotland Yard enclosed an optician's specification identical with that sent by Mr Crimplesham, and added that it was an unusual one, owing to the peculiar strength of the lenses and the marked difference between the sight of the two eyes.

'That's good enough,' said Parker.

'Yes,' said Wimsey. 'Then Possibility No. 3 is knocked on the head. There remain Possibility No. 1: Accident or Misunderstanding, and No. 2: Deliberate Villainy, of a remarkably bold and calculating kind — of a kind, in fact, characteristic of the author or authors of our two problems. Following the methods inculcated at that University of which I have the honour to be a member, we will now examine severally the various suggestions afforded by Possibility No. 2. This Possibility may be again sub-divided into two or more Hypotheses. On Hypothesis 1 (strongly advocated by my distinguished colleague Professor Snupshed), the criminal, whom we may designate as X, is not identical with Crimplesham, but is using the name of Crimplesham as his shield, or aegis. This hypothesis may be further sub-divided into two alternatives. Alternative A: Crimplesham is an innocent and unconscious accomplice, and X is in his employment. X writes in Crimplesham's name on Crimplesham's office-paper and obtains that the object in question, i.e. the eye-glasses, be despatched to Crimplesham's address. He is in a position to intercept the parcel before it reaches Crimplesham. The presumption is that X is Crimplesham's charwoman, office-boy, clerk, secretary or porter. This offers a wide field of investigation. The method of inquiry will be to interview Crimplesham and discover whether he sent the letter, and if not, who has access to his correspondence. Alternative B: Crimplesham is under X's influence or in his power, and has been induced to write the letter by *(a)* bribery, *(b)* misrepresentation or *(c)* threats. X may in that case be a persuasive relation or friend, or else a creditor, blackmailer or assassin; Crimplesham, on the other hand, is obviously venal or a fool. The method of inquiry in this case, I would tentatively suggest, is again to interview Crimplesham, put the facts of the case strongly before him, and assure him in the most intimidating terms that he is liable to a prolonged term of penal servitude as an accessory after the fact in the crime of murder — Ah-hem! Trusting gentlemen, that you have followed me thus far, we will pass to the consideration of Hypothesis No. 2, to which I personally incline, and according to which X is identical with Crimplesham.

'In this case, Crimplesham, who is, in the

words of an English classic, a man-of-infinite-resource-and-sagacity, correctly deduces that, of all people, the last whom we shall expect to find answering our advertisement is the criminal himself. Accordingly, he plays a bold game of bluff. He invents an occasion on which the glasses may very easily have been lost or stolen, and applies for them. If confronted, nobody will be more astonished than he to learn where they were found. He will produce witnesses to prove that he left Victoria at 5.45 and emerged from the train at Balham at the scheduled time, and sat up all Monday night playing chess with a respectable gentleman well known in Balham. In this case, the method of inquiry will be to pump the respectable gentleman in Balham, and if he should happen to be a single gentleman with a deaf housekeeper, it may be no easy matter to impugn the alibi, since, outside detective romances, few ticket-collectors and bus-conductors keep an exact remembrance of all the passengers passing between Balham and London on any and every evening of the week.

'Finally, gentlemen, I will frankly point out the weak point of all these hypotheses, namely: that none of them offers any explanation as to why the incriminating article was left so conspicuously on the body in the first instance.'

Mr Parker had listened with commendable patience to this academic exposition.

'Might not X,' he suggested, 'be an enemy of Crimplesham's, who designed to throw suspicion upon him?'

'He might. In that case he should be easy to

discover, since he obviously lives in close proximity to Crimplesham and his glasses, and Crimplesham in fear of his life will then be a valuable ally for the prosecution.'

'How about the first possibility of all, misunderstanding or accident?'

'Well! Well, for purposes of discussion, nothing, because it really doesn't afford any data for discussion.'

'In any case,' said Parker, 'the obvious course appears to be to go to Salisbury.'

'That seems indicated,' said Lord Peter.

'Very well,' said the detective, 'is it to be you or me or both of us?'

'It is to be me,' said Lord Peter, 'and that for two reasons. First, because, if (by Possibility No. 2, Hypothesis 1, Alternative A) Crimplesham is an innocent cat's paw, the person who put in the advertisement is the proper person to hand over the property. Secondly, because, if we are to adopt Hypothesis 2, we must not overlook the sinister possibility that Crimplesham-X is laying a careful trap to rid himself of the person who so unwarily advertised in the daily press his interest in the solution of the Battersea Park mystery.'

'That appears to me to be an argument for our both going,' objected the detective.

'Far from it,' said Lord Peter. 'Why play into the hands of Crimplesham-X by delivering over to him the only two men in London with the evidence, such as it is, and shall I say the wits, to connect him with the Battersea body?'

'But if we told the Yard where we were going, and we both got nobbled,' said Mr Parker, 'it would afford strong presumptive evidence of Crimplesham's guilt, and anyhow, if he didn't get hanged for murdering the man in the bath he'd at least get hanged for murdering us.'

'Well,' said Lord Peter, 'if he only murdered me you could still hang him — what's the good of wasting a sound, marriageable young male like yourself? Besides, how about old Levy? If you're incapacitated, do you think anybody else is going to find him?'

'But we could frighten Crimplesham by threatening him with the Yard.'

'Well, dash it all, if it comes to that, *I* can frighten him by threatening him with *you*, which, seeing you hold what evidence there is, is much more to the point. And, then, suppose it's a wild-goose chase after all, you'll have wasted time when you might have been getting on with the case. There are several things that need doing.'

'Well,' said Parker, silenced but reluctant, 'why can't I go, in that case?'

'Bosh!' said Lord Peter. 'I am retained (by old Mrs Thipps, for whom I entertain the greatest respect) to deal with this case, and it's only by courtesy I allow you to have anything to do with it.'

Mr Parker groaned.

'Will you at least take Bunter?' he said.

'In deference to your feelings,' replied Lord Peter, 'I will take Bunter, though he could be far more usefully employed taking photographs or overhauling my wardrobe. When is there a good train to Salisbury, Bunter?'

91

'There is an excellent train at 10.50, my lord.'

'Kindly make arrangements to catch it,' said Lord Peter, throwing off his bathrobe and trailing away with it into his bedroom. 'And Parker — if you have nothing else to do you might get hold of Levy's secretary and look into that little matter of the Peruvian oil.'

★   ★   ★

Lord Peter took with him, for light reading in the train, Sir Reuben Levy's diary. It was a simple, and in the light of recent facts, rather a pathetic document. The terrible fighter of the Stock Exchange, who could with one nod set the surly bear dancing, or bring the savage bull to feed out of his hand, whose breath devastated whole districts with famine or swept financial potentates from their seats, was revealed in private life as kindly, domestic, innocently proud of himself and his belongings, confiding, generous and a little dull. His own small economies were duly chronicled side by side with extravagant presents to his wife and daughter. Small incidents of household routine appeared, such as: 'Man came to mend the conservatory roof,' or 'The new butler (Simpson) has arrived, recommended by the Goldbergs. I think he will be satisfactory.' All visitors and entertainments were duly entered, from a very magnificent lunch to Lord Dewsbury, the Ministry for Foreign Affairs, and Dr Jabez K. Wort, the American plenipotentiary, through a series of diplomatic dinners to eminent financiers, down to intimate family

92

gatherings of persons designated by Christian names or nicknames. About May there came a mention of Lady Levy's nerves, and further reference was made to the subject in subsequent months. In September it was stated that 'Freke came to see my dear wife and advised complete rest and change of scene. She thinks of going abroad with Rachel.' The name of the famous nerve-specialist occurred as a diner or luncher about once a month, and it came into Lord Peter's mind that Freke would be a good person to consult about Levy himself. 'People sometimes tell things to the doctor,' he murmured to himself. 'And, by Jove! If Levy was simply going round to see Freke on Monday night, that rather disposes of the Battersea incident, doesn't it?' He made a note to look up Sir Julian and turned on further. On September 18th, Lady Levy and her daughter had left for the south of France. Then suddenly, under the date October 5th, Lord Peter found what he was looking for: 'Goldberg, Skriner and Milligan to dinner.'

There was the evidence that Milligan had been in that house. There had been a formal entertainment — a meeting as of two duellists shaking hands before the fight. Skriner was a well-known picture-dealer; Lord Peter imagined an after-dinner excursion upstairs to see the two Corots in the drawing-room, and the portrait of the eldest Levy girl, who had died at the age of sixteen. It was by Augustus John, and hung in the bedroom. The name of the red-haired secretary was nowhere mentioned, unless the initial S., occurring in another entry, referred to him. Throughout September and October Anderson (of Wyndham's) had been a frequent visitor.

Lord Peter shook his head over the diary, and turned to the consideration of the Battersea Park mystery. Whereas in the Levy affair it was easy enough to supply a motive for the crime, if crime it were, and the difficulty was to discover the method of its carrying out and the whereabouts of the victim, in the other case the chief obstacle to inquiry was the entire absence of any imaginable motive. It was odd that, although the papers had carried news of the affair from one end of the country to the other and a description of the body had been sent to every police station in the country, nobody had as yet come forward to identify the mysterious occupant of Mr Thipps's bath. It was true that the description, which mentioned the clean-shaven chin, elegantly cut hair and the pince-nez, was rather misleading, but on the other hand, the police had managed to discover the number of molars missing, and the height, complexion and other data were correctly enough stated, as also the date at which death had presumably occurred. It seemed, however, as though the man had melted out of society without leaving a gap or so much as a ripple. Assigning a motive for the murder of a person without relations or antecedents or even clothes is like trying to visualise the fourth dimension — admirable exercise for the imagination, but arduous and inconclusive. Even if the day's interview should disclose black spots in the past or present of Mr Crimplesham, how were they to be brought into connection with a person apparently without a past, and whose present was confined to the narrow limits of a bath and a police mortuary?

'Bunter,' said Lord Peter, 'I beg that in the future you will restrain me from starting two hares at once. These cases are gettin' to be a strain on my constitution. One hare has nowhere to run from, and the other has nowhere to run to. It's a kind of mental D.T., Bunter. When this is over I shall turn pussyfoot, forswear the police news, and take to an emollient diet of the works of the late Charles Garvice.'

★   ★   ★

It was its comparative proximity to Milford Hill that induced Lord Peter to lunch at the Minster Hotel rather than at the White Hart or some other more picturesquely situated hostel. It was not a lunch calculated to cheer his mind; as in all Cathedral cities, the atmosphere of the Close pervades every nook and corner of Salisbury, and no food in that city but seems faintly flavoured with prayer-books. As he sat sadly consuming that impassive pale substance known to the English as 'cheese' unqualified (for there are cheeses which go openly by their names, as Stilton, Camembert, Gruyère, Wensleydale or Gorgonzola, but 'cheese' is cheese and every-where the same), he inquired of the waiter the whereabouts of Mr Crimplesham's office.

The waiter directed him to a house rather

farther up the street on the opposite side, adding: 'But anybody'll tell you, sir; Mr Crimplesham's very well known hereabouts.'

'He's a good solicitor, I suppose?' said Lord Peter.

'Oh, yes, sir,' said the waiter, 'you couldn't do better than trust to Mr Crimplesham, sir. There's folk say he's old-fashioned, but I'd rather have my little bit of business done by Mr Crimplesham than by one of these fly-away young men. Not but what Mr Crimplesham'll be retiring soon, sir, I don't doubt, for he must be close on eighty, sir, if he's a day, but then there's young Mr Wicks to carry on the business, and he's a very nice, steady-like young gentleman.'

'Is Mr Crimplesham really as old as that?' said Lord Peter. 'Dear me! He must be very active for his years. A friend of mine was doing business with him in town last week.'

'Wonderful active, sir,' agreed the waiter, 'and with his game leg, too, you'd be surprised. But there, sir, I often think when a man's once past a certain age, the older he grows the tougher he gets, and women the same or more so.'

'Very likely,' said Lord Peter, calling up and dismissing the mental picture of a gentleman of eighty with a game leg carrying a dead body over the roof of a Battersea flat at midnight. ' "He's tough, sir, tough, is old Joey Bag-stock, tough and devilish sly," ' he added thoughtlessly.

'Indeed, sir?' said the waiter. 'I couldn't say, I'm sure.'

'I beg your pardon,' said Lord Peter. 'I was quoting poetry. Very silly of me. I got the habit at

96

my mother's knee and I can't break myself of it.'

'No, sir,' said the waiter, pocketing a liberal tip. 'Thank you very much, sir. You'll find the house easy. Just afore you come to Penny-farthing Street, sir, about two turnings off, on the right hand side opposite.'

'Afraid that disposes of Crimplesham-X,' said Lord Peter. 'I'm rather sorry; he was a fine sinister figure as I had pictured him. Still, his may yet be the brain behind the hands — the aged spider sitting invisible in the centre of the vibrating web, you know, Bunter.'

'Yes, my lord,' said Bunter. They were walking up the street together.

'There is the office over the way,' pursued Lord Peter. 'I think, Bunter, you might step into this little shop and purchase a sporting paper, and if I do not emerge from the villain's lair — say within three-quarters of an hour, you may take such steps as your perspicuity may suggest.'

Mr Bunter turned into the shop as desired, and Lord Peter walked across and rang the lawyer's bell with decision.

'The truth, the whole truth and nothing but the truth is my long suit here, I fancy,' he murmured, and when the door was opened by a clerk he delivered over his card with an unflinching air.

He was ushered immediately into a confidential-looking office, obviously furnished in the early years of Queen Victoria's reign, and never altered since. A lean, frail-looking old gentleman rose briskly from his chair as he entered and limped forward to meet him.

'My dear sir,' exclaimed the lawyer, 'how extremely good of you to come in person! Indeed, I am ashamed to have given you so much trouble. I trust you were passing this way, and that my glasses have not put you to any great inconvenience. Pray take a seat, Lord Peter.' He peered gratefully at the young man over a pince-nez obviously the fellow of that now adorning a dossier in Scotland Yard.

Lord Peter sat down. The lawyer sat down. Lord Peter picked up a glass paper-weight from the desk and weighed it thoughtfully in his hand. Subconsciously he noted what an admirable set of finger-prints he was leaving upon it. He replaced it with precision on the exact centre of a pile of letters.

'It's quite all right,' said Lord Peter. 'I was here on business. Very happy to be of service to you. Very awkward to lose one's glasses, Mr Crimplesham.'

'Yes,' said the lawyer, 'I assure you I feel quite lost without them. I have this pair, but they do not fit my nose so well — besides, that chain has a great sentimental value for me. I was terribly distressed on arriving at Balham to find that I had lost them. I made inquiries of the railway, but to no purpose. I feared they had been stolen. There were such crowds at Victoria, and the carriage was packed with people all the way to Balham. Did you come across them in the train?'

'Well, no,' said Lord Peter. 'I found them in rather an unexpected place. Do you mind telling me if you recognised any of your fellow-travellers on that occasion?'

The lawyer stared at him.

'Not a soul,' he answered. 'Why do you ask?'

'Well,' said Lord Peter. 'I thought perhaps the — the person with whom I found them might have taken them for a joke.'

The lawyer looked puzzled.

'Did the person claim to be an acquaintance of mine?' he inquired. 'I know practically nobody in London, except the friend with whom I was staying in Balham, Dr Philpots, and I should be very greatly surprised at his practising a jest upon me. He knew very well how distressed I was at the loss of the glasses. My business was to attend a meeting of shareholders in Medlicott's Bank, but the other gentlemen present were all personally unknown to me, and I cannot think that any of them would take so great a liberty. In any case,' he added, 'as the glasses are here, I will not inquire too closely into the manner of their restoration. I am deeply obliged to you for your trouble.'

Lord Peter hesitated.

'Pray forgive my seeming inquisitiveness,' he said, 'but I must ask you another question. It sounds rather melodramatic, I'm afraid, but it's this. Are you aware that you have any enemy — anyone, I mean, who would profit by your — er — decease or disgrace?'

Mr Crimplesham sat frozen into stony surprise and disapproval.

'May I ask the meaning of this extraordinary question?' he inquired stiffly.

'Well,' said Lord Peter, 'the circumstances are a little unusual. You may recollect that my advertisement was addressed to the jeweller who sold the chain.'

'That surprised me at the time,' said Mr Crimplesham, 'but I begin to think your advertisement and your behaviour are all of a piece.'

'They are,' said Lord Peter. 'As a matter of fact I did not expect the owner of the glasses to answer my advertisement. Mr Crimplesham, you have no doubt read what the papers have to say about the Battersea Park mystery. Your glasses are the pair that was found on the body, and they are now in the possession of the police at Scotland Yard, as you may see by this.' He placed the specification of the glasses and the official note before Crimplesham.

'Good God!' exclaimed the lawyer. He glanced at the paper, and then looked narrowly at Lord Peter.

'Are you yourself connected with the police?' he inquired.

'Not officially,' said Lord Peter. 'I am investigating the matter privately, in the interests of one of the parties.'

Mr Crimplesham rose to his feet.

'My good man,' he said, 'this is a very impudent attempt, but blackmail is an indictable offence, and I advise you to leave my office before you commit yourself.' He rang the bell.

'I was afraid you'd take it like that,' said Lord Peter. 'It looks as though this ought to have been my friend Detective Parker's job, after all.' He laid Parker's card on the table beside the specification, and added: 'If you should wish to see me again, Mr Crimplesham, before tomorrow morning, you will find me at the Minster Hotel.'

Mr Crimplesham disdained to reply further than to direct the clerk who entered to 'show this person out'.

In the entrance Lord Peter brushed against a tall young man who was just coming in, and who stared at him with surprised recognition. His face, however, aroused no memories in Lord Peter's mind, and that baffled gentleman, calling out Bunter from the newspaper shop, departed to his hotel to get a trunk-call through to Parker.

Meanwhile in the office, the meditations of the indignant Mr Crimplesham were interrupted by the entrance of his junior partner.

'I say,' said the latter, 'has somebody done something really wicked at last? Whatever brings such a distinguished amateur of crime on our sober doorstep?'

'I have been the victim of a vulgar attempt at blackmail,' said the lawyer, 'an individual passing himself off as Lord Peter Wimsey — '

'But that *is* Lord Peter Wimsey,' said Mr Wicks, 'there's no mistaking him. I saw him give evidence in the Attenbury emerald case. He's a big little pot in his way, you know, and goes fishing with the head of Scotland Yard.'

'Oh dear,' said Mr Crimplesham.

* * *

Fate arranged that the nerves of Mr Crimplesham should be tried that afternoon. When, escorted by Mr Wicks, he arrived at the Minster Hotel, he was informed by the porter that Lord Peter Wimsey had strolled out, mentioning that he thought of attending Evensong. 'But his man is here, sir,' he added, 'if you like to leave a message.'

Mr Wicks thought that on the whole it would be well to leave a message. Mr Bunter, on inquiry, was found to be sitting by the telephone, waiting for a trunk-call. As Mr Wicks addressed him the bell rang, and Mr Bunter, politely excusing himself, took down the receiver.

'Hullo!' he said. 'Is that Mr Parker? Oh, thanks? Exchange! Exchange? Sorry, can you put me through to Scotland Yard? Excuse me, gentlemen, keeping you waiting — Exchange! all right — Scotland Yard — Hullo! Is that Scotland Yard? — Is Inspector Parker round there? — Can I speak to him? — I shall have done in a moment, gentlemen. — Hullo! is that you, Mr Parker? Lord Peter would be much obliged if you could find it convenient to step down to Salisbury, sir. Oh, no, sir, he's in excellent health, sir — just stepped round to hear Evensong, sir — oh, no, I think tomorrow morning would do excellently, sir, thank you, sir.'

6

It was, in fact, inconvenient for Mr Parker to leave London. He had had to go and see Lady Levy towards the end of the morning, and subsequently his plans for the day had been thrown out of gear and his movements delayed by the discovery that the adjourned inquest on Mr Thipps's unknown visitor was to be held that afternoon, since nothing very definite seemed forthcoming from Inspector Sugg's inquiries. Jury and witnesses had been convened accordingly for three o'clock. Mr Parker might altogether have missed the event, had he not run against Sugg that morning at the Yard and extracted the information from him as one would a reluctant tooth. Inspector Sugg, indeed, considered Mr Parker rather interfering; moreover, he was hand-in-glove with Lord Peter Wimsey, and Inspector Sugg had no words for the interferingness of Lord Peter. He could not, however, when directly questioned, deny that there was to be an inquest that afternoon, nor could he prevent Mr Parker from enjoying the inalienable right of any interested British citizen to be present. At a little before three, therefore, Mr Parker was in his place, and amusing himself with watching the efforts of those persons who arrived after the room was packed to insinuate, bribe or bully themselves into a position of vantage. The Coroner, a medical man of precise habits and unimaginative aspect, arrived punctually, and looking peevishly round at the crowded assembly, directed all the windows to be opened, thus letting in a stream of drizzling fog upon the heads of the unfortunates on that side of the room. This caused a commotion and some expressions of disapproval, checked sternly by the Coroner, who said that with the influenza about again an unventilated room was a death-trap; that anybody who chose to object to open windows had the obvious remedy of leaving the court, and further, that if any disturbance was made he would clear the court. He then took a Formamint lozenge, and proceeded, after the usual preliminaries, to call up fourteen good and lawful persons and swear them diligently to inquire and a true presentment make of all matters touching the death of the gentleman with the pince-nez and to give a true verdict according to the evidence, so help them God. When an expostulation by a woman juror — an elderly lady in spectacles who kept a sweet-shop, and appeared to wish she was back there — had been summarily squashed by the Coroner, the jury departed to view the body. Mr Parker gazed round again and identified the unhappy Mr Thipps and the girl Gladys led into an adjoining room under the grim guard of the police. They were soon followed by a gaunt old lady in a bonnet and mantle. With her, in a wonderful fur coat and a motor bonnet of fascinating construction, came the Dowager Duchess of Denver, her quick, dark eyes darting hither and thither about the crowd. The next moment they

104

had lighted on Mr Parker, who had several times visited the Dower House, and she nodded to him, and spoke to a policeman. Before long, a way opened magically through the press, and Mr Parker found himself accommodated with a front seat just behind the Duchess, who greeted him charmingly, and said: 'What's happened to poor Peter?' Parker began to explain, and the Coroner glanced irritably in their direction. Somebody went up and whispered in his ear, at which he coughed, and took another Formamint.

'We came up by car,' said the Duchess — 'so tiresome — such bad roads between Denver and Gunbury St Walters — and there were people coming to lunch — I had to put them off — I couldn't let the old lady go alone, could I? By the way, such an odd thing's happened about the Church Restoration Fund — the Vicar — oh, dear, here are these people coming back again; well, I'll tell you afterwards — do look at that woman looking shocked, and the girl in tweeds trying to look as if she sat on undraped gentlemen every day of her life — I don't mean that — corpses of course — but one finds oneself being so Elizabethan nowadays — what an awful little man the Coroner is, isn't he? He's looking daggers at me — do you think he'll dare to clear me out of the court or commit me for what-you-may-call-it?'

The first part of the evidence was not of great interest to Mr Parker. The wretched Mr Thipps, who had caught cold in gaol, deposed in an unhappy croak to having discovered the body, when he went to take his bath at eight o'clock.

He had had such a shock, he had to sit down and send the girl for brandy. He had never seen the deceased before. He had no idea how he came there.

Yes, he had been in Manchester the day before. He had arrived at St Pancras at ten o'clock. He had cloak-roomed his bag. At this point Mr Thipps became very red, unhappy and confused, and glanced nervously about the court.

'Now, Mr Thipps,' said the Coroner, briskly, 'we must have your movements quite clear. You must appreciate the importance of the matter. You have chosen to give evidence, which you need not have done, but having done so, you will find it best to be perfectly explicit.'

'Yes,' said Mr Thipps faintly.

'Have you cautioned this witness, officer?' inquired the Coroner, turning sharply to Inspector Sugg.

The Inspector replied that he had told Mr Thipps that anything he said might be used agin' him at his trial. Mr Thipps became ashy, and said in a bleating voice that he 'adn't — hadn't meant to do anything that wasn't right.

This remark produced a mild sensation, and the Coroner became even more acidulated in manner than before.

'Is anybody representing Mr Thipps?' he asked, irritably. 'No? Did you not explain to him that he could — that he *ought* to be represented? You did not? Really, Inspector! Did you not know, Mr Thipps, that you had a right to be legally represented?'

Mr Thipps clung to a chair-back for support, and said 'No' in a voice barely audible.

'It is incredible,' said the Coroner, 'that so-called educated people should be so ignorant of the legal procedure of their own country. This places us in a very awkward position. I doubt, Inspector, whether I should permit the prisoner — Mr Thipps — to give evidence at all. It is a delicate position.'

The perspiration stood on Mr Thipps's forehead.

'Save us from our friends,' whispered the Duchess to Parker. 'If that cough-drop-devouring creature had openly instructed those fourteen people — and what unfinished-looking faces they have — so characteristic, I always think, of the lower middle-class, rather like sheep, or calves' head (boiled, I mean), to bring in wilful murder against the poor little man, he couldn't have made himself plainer.'

'He can't let him incriminate himself, you know,' said Parker.

'Stuff!' said the Duchess. 'How could the man incriminate himself when he never did anything in his life? You men never think of anything but your red tape.'

Meanwhile Mr Thipps, wiping his brow with a handkerchief, had summoned up courage. He stood up with a kind of weak dignity, like a small white rabbit brought to bay.

'I would rather tell you,' he said, 'though it's reely very unpleasant for a man in my position. But I reely couldn't have it thought for a moment that I'd committed this dreadful crime.

I assure you, gentlemen, I *couldn't bear* that. No. I'd rather tell you the truth, though I'm afraid it places me in rather a — well, I'll tell you.'

'You fully understand the gravity of making such a statement, Mr Thipps,' said the Coroner.

'Quite,' said Mr Thipps. 'It's all right — I — might I have a drink of water?'

'Take your time,' said the Coroner, at the same time robbing his remark of all conviction by an impatient glance at his watch.

'Thank you, sir,' said Mr Thipps. 'Well, then, it's true I got to St Pancras at ten. But there was a man in the carriage with me. He'd got in at Leicester. I didn't recognise him at first, but he turned out to be an old school-fellow of mine.'

'What was this gentleman's name?' inquired the Coroner, his pencil poised.

Mr Thipps shrank together visibly.

'I'm afraid I can't tell you that,' he said. 'You see — that is, you *will* see — it would get him into trouble, and I couldn't do that — no, I reely couldn't do that, not if any life depended on it. No!' he added, as the ominous pertinence of the last phrase smote upon him. 'I'm sure I couldn't do that.'

'Well, well,' said the Coroner.

The Duchess leaned over to Parker again. 'I'm beginning quite to admire the little man,' she said.

Mr Thipps resumed.

'When we got to St Pancras I was going home, but my friend said no. We hadn't met for a long time and we ought to — to make a night of it, was his expression. I fear I was weak, and let him

108

over-persuade me to accompany him to one of his haunts. I use the word advisedly,' said Mr Thipps, 'and I assure you, sir, that if I had known beforehand where we were going I never would have set foot in the place.

'I cloak-roomed my bag, for he did not like the notion of our being encumbered with it, and we got into a taxi-cab and drove to the corner of Tottenham Court Road and Oxford Street. We then walked a little way, and turned into a side street (I do not recollect which) where there was an open door, with the light shining out. There was a man at a counter, and my friend bought some tickets, and I heard the man at the counter say something to him about 'Your friend,' meaning me, and my friend said, 'Oh, yes, he's been here before, haven't you, Alf?' (which was what they called me at school), though I assure you, sir' — here Mr Thipps grew very earnest — 'I never had, and nothing in the world should induce me to go to such a place again.

'Well, we went down into a room underneath, where there were drinks, and my friend had several, and made me take one or two — though I am an abstemious man as a rule — and he talked to some other men and girls who were there — a very vulgar set of people, I thought them, though I wouldn't say but what some of the young ladies were nice-looking enough. One of them sat on my friend's knee and called him a slow old thing, and told him to come on — so we went into another room, where there were a lot of people dancing all these up-to-date dances. My friend went and danced, and I sat on the sofa. One of the young ladies came up to me and said, didn't I dance, and I said 'No', so she said wouldn't I stand her a drink then. 'You'll stand us a drink then, darling,' that was what she said, and I said, 'Wasn't it after hours?' and she said that didn't matter. So I ordered the drink — a gin and bitters it was — for I didn't like not to, the young lady seemed to expect it of me and I felt it wouldn't be gentlemanly to refuse when she asked. But it went against my conscience — such a young girl as she was — and she put her arm round my neck afterwards and kissed me just like as if she was paying for the drink — and it reely went to my 'eart,' said Mr Thipps, a little ambiguously, but with uncommon emphasis.

Here somebody at the back said, 'Cheer-oh' and a sound was heard as of the noisy smacking of lips.

'Remove the person who made that improper noise,' said the Coroner, with great indignation. 'Go on, please, Mr Thipps.'

'Well,' said Mr Thipps, 'about half-past twelve, as I should reckon, things began to get a bit lively, and I was looking for my friend to say good-night, not wishing to stay longer, as you will understand, when I saw him with one of the young ladies, and they seemed to be getting on altogether too well, if you follow me, my friend pulling the ribbons off her shoulder and the young lady laughing — and so on,' said Mr Thipps, hurriedly, 'so I thought I'd just slip quietly out, when I heard a scuffle and a shout — and before I knew what was happening there

110

were half a dozen policemen in, and the lights went out, and everybody stampeding and shouting — quite horrid, it was. I was knocked down in the rush, and hit my head a nasty knock on a chair — that was where I got that bruise they asked me about — and I was dreadfully afraid I'd never get away and it would all come out, and perhaps my photograph in the papers, when someone caught hold of me — I think it was the young lady I'd given the gin and bitters to — and she said, 'This way', and pushed me along a passage and out at the back somewhere. So I ran through some streets, and found myself in Goodge Street, and there I got a taxi and came home. I saw the account of the raid afterwards in the papers, and saw my friend had escaped, and so, as it wasn't the sort of thing I wanted made public, and I didn't want to get him into difficulties, I just said nothing. But that's the truth.'

'Well, Mr Thipps,' said the Coroner, 'we shall be able to substantiate a certain amount of this story. Your friend's name — '

'No,' said Mr Thipps, stoutly, 'not on any account.'

'Very good,' said the Coroner. 'Now, can you tell us what time you did get in?'

'About half-past one, I should think. Though reely, I was so upset — '

'Quite so. Did you go straight to bed?'

'Yes, I took my sandwich and glass of milk first. I thought it might settle my inside, so to speak,' added the witness, apologetically, 'not being accustomed to alcohol so late at night and

111

on an empty stomach, as you may say.'

'Quite so. Nobody sat up for you?'

'Nobody.'

'How long did you take getting into bed first and last?'

Mr Thipps thought it might have been half an hour.

'Did you visit the bathroom before turning in?'

'No.'

'And you heard nothing in the night?'

'No. I fell fast asleep. I was rather agitated, so I took a little dose to make me sleep, and what with being so tired and the milk and the dose, I just tumbled right off and didn't wake till Gladys called me.'

Further questioning elicited little from Mr Thipps. Yes, the bathroom window had been open when he went in in the morning, he was sure of that, and he had spoken very sharply to the girl about it. He was ready to answer any questions; he would be only too 'appy — happy to have this dreadful affair sifted to the bottom.

Gladys Horrocks stated that she had been in Mr Thipps's employment about three months. Her previous employers would speak to her character. It was her duty to make the round of the flat at night, when she had seen Mrs Thipps to bed at ten. Yes, she remembered doing so on Monday evening. She had looked into all the rooms. Did she recollect shutting the bathroom window that night? Well, no, she couldn't swear to it, not in particular, but when Mr Thipps called her into the bathroom in the morning it certainly *was* open. She had not been into the

112

bathroom before Mr Thipps went in. Well, yes, it had happened that she had left that window open before, when anyone had been 'aving a bath in the evening and 'ad left the blind down. Mrs Thipps 'ad 'ad a bath on Monday evening. Mondays was one of her regular bath nights. She was very much afraid she 'adn't shut the window on Monday night, though she wished her 'ead 'ad been cut off afore she'd been so forgetful.

Here the witness burst into tears and was given some water, while the Coroner refreshed himself with a third lozenge.

Recovering, witness stated that she had certainly looked into all the rooms before going to bed. No, it was quite impossible for a body to be 'idden in the flat without her seeing of it. She 'ad been in the kitchen all evening, and there wasn't 'ardly room to keep the best dinner service there, let alone a body. Old Mrs Thipps sat in the drawing-room. Yes, she was sure she'd been into the dining-room. How? Because she put Mr Thipps's milk and sandwiches there ready for him. There had been nothing in there — that she could swear to. Nor yet in her own bedroom, nor in the 'all. Had she searched the bedroom cupboard and the box-room? Well, no, not to say searched; she wasn't used to searchin' people's 'ouses for skeletons every night. So that a man might have concealed himself in the box-room or a wardrobe? She supposed he might.

In reply to a woman juror — well, yes, she was walking out with a young man. Williams was his name, Bill Williams — well, yes, William Williams, if they insisted. He was a glazier by profession. Well, yes, he 'ad been in the flat sometimes. Well, she supposed you might say he was acquainted with the flat. Had she ever — no, she 'adn't and if she'd thought such a question was going to be put to a respectable girl she wouldn't 'ave offered to give evidence. The vicar of St Mary's would speak to her character and to Mr Williams's. Last time Mr Williams was at the flat was a fortnight ago.

Well, no, it wasn't exactly the last time she 'ad seen Mr Williams. Well, yes, the last time was Monday — well, yes, Monday night. Well, if she must tell the truth, she must. Yes, the officer had cautioned her, but there wasn't any 'arm in it, and it was better to lose her place than to be 'ung, though it was a cruel shame a girl couldn't 'ave a bit of fun without a nasty corpse comin' in through the window to get 'er into difficulties. After she 'ad put Mr Thipps to bed, she 'ad slipped out to go to the Plumbers' and Glaziers' Ball at the 'Black Faced Ram'. Mr Williams 'ad met 'er and brought 'er back. 'E could testify for where she'd been and that there wasn't no 'arm in it. She'd left before the end of the ball. It might 'ave been two o'clock when she got back. She'd got the keys of the flat from Mrs Thipps's drawer when Mrs Thipps wasn't looking. She 'ad asked leave to go, but couldn't get it, along of Mr Thipps bein' away that night. She was bitterly sorry she 'ad be'aved so, and she was sure she'd been punished for it. She had 'eard nothing suspicious when she came in. She had gone straight to bed without looking round the flat. She wished she were dead.

No, Mr and Mrs Thipps didn't 'ardly ever 'ave any visitors: they kep' themselves very retired. She had found the outside door bolted that morning as usual. She wouldn't never believe any 'arm of Mr Thipps. Thank you, Miss Horrocks. Call Georgiana Thipps, and the Coroner thought we had better light the gas.

The examination of Mrs Thipps provided more entertainment than enlightenment, affording as it did an excellent example of the game called 'cross questions and crooked answers'. After fifteen minutes' suffering, both in voice and temper, the Coroner abandoned the struggle, leaving the lady with the last word.

'You needn't try to bully me, young man,' said that octogenarian with spirit, 'settin' there spoilin' your stomach with them nasty jujubes.'

At this point a young man arose in court and demanded to give evidence. Having explained that he was William Williams, glazier, he was sworn, and corroborated the evidence of Gladys Horrocks in the matter of her presence at the 'Black Faced Ram' on the Monday night. They had returned to the flat rather before two, he thought, but certainly later than 1.30. He was sorry that he had persuaded Miss Horrocks to come out with him when she didn't ought. He had observed nothing of a suspicious nature in Prince of Wales Road at either visit.

Inspector Sugg gave evidence of having been called in at about half-past eight on Tuesday morning. He had considered the girl's manner to be suspicious and had arrested her. On later information, leading him to suspect that the deceased might have been murdered that night, he had arrested Mr Thipps. He had found no trace of breaking into the flat. There were marks on the bathroom window-sill which pointed to somebody having got in that way. There were no ladder marks or footmarks in the yard; the yard was paved with asphalt. He had examined the roof, but found nothing on the roof. In his opinion the body had been brought into the flat previously and concealed till the evening by someone who had then gone out during the night by the bathroom window, with the connivance of the girl. In that case, why should not the girl have let the person out by the door? Well, it might have been so. Had he found traces of a body or a man or both having been hidden in the flat? He found nothing to show that they might *not* have been so concealed. What was the evidence that led him to suppose that the death had occurred that night?

At this point Inspector Sugg appeared uneasy, and endeavoured to retire upon his professional dignity. On being pressed, however, he admitted that the evidence in question had come to nothing.

One of the jurors: Was it the case that any fingermarks had been left by the criminal?

Some marks had been found on the bath, but the criminal had worn gloves.

The Coroner: Do you draw any conclusion from this fact as to the experience of the criminal?

116

Inspector Sugg: Looks as if he was an old hand, sir.

The Juror: Is that very consistent with the charge against Alfred Thipps, Inspector?

The Inspector was silent.

The Coroner: In the light of the evidence which you have just heard, do you still press the charge against Alfred Thipps and Gladys Horrocks?

Inspector Sugg: I consider the whole set-out highly suspicious. Thipps's story isn't corroborated, and as for the girl Horrocks, how do we know this Williams ain't in it as well?

William Williams: Now, you drop that. I can bring a 'undred witnesses —

The Coroner: Silence, if you please. I am surprised, Inspector, that you should make this suggestion in that manner. It is highly improper. By the way, can you tell us whether a police raid was actually carried out on the Monday night on any Night Club in the neighbourhood of St Giles's Circus?

Inspector Sugg: (sulkily): I believe there was something of the sort.

The Coroner: You will, no doubt, inquire into the matter. I seem to recollect having seen some mention of it in the newspapers. Thank you, Inspector, that will do.

Several witnesses having appeared and testified to the characters of Mr Thipps and Gladys Horrocks, the Coroner stated his intention of proceeding to the medical evidence.

'Sir Julian Freke.'

There was considerable stir in the court as the

117

great specialist walked up to give evidence. He was not only a distinguished man, but a striking figure, with his wide shoulders, upright carriage and leonine head. His manner as he kissed the Book presented to him with the usual deprecatory mumble by the Coroner's officer, was that of a St Paul condescending to humour the timid mumbo-jumbo of superstitious Corinthians.

'So handsome, I always think,' whispered the Duchess to Mr Parker, 'just exactly like William Morris, with that bush of hair and beard and those exciting eyes looking out of it — so splendid, these dear men always devoted to something or other — not but what I think socialism is a mistake — of course it works with all those nice people, too good and happy in art linen and the weather always perfect — Morris, I mean, you know — but so difficult in real life. Science is different — I'm sure if I had nerves I should go to Sir Julian just to look at him — eyes like that give one something to think about, and that's what most of these people want, only I never had any — nerves, I mean. Don't you think so?'

'You are Sir Julian Freke,' said the Coroner, 'and live at St Luke's House, Prince of Wales Road, Battersea, where you exercise a general direction over the surgical side of St Luke's Hospital?'

Sir Julian assented briefly to this definition of his personality.

'You were the first medical man to see the deceased?'

'I was.'

'And you have since conducted an examination in collaboration with Dr Grimbold of Scotland Yard?'

'I have.'

'You are in agreement as to the cause of death?'

'Generally speaking, yes.'

'Will you communicate your impressions to the jury?'

'I was engaged in research work in the dissecting-room at St Luke's Hospital at about nine o'clock on Monday morning, when I was informed that Inspector Sugg wished to see me. He told me that the dead body of a man had been discovered under mysterious circumstances at 59 Queen Caroline Mansions. He asked me whether it could be supposed to be a joke perpetrated by any of the medical students at the hospital. I was able to assure him, by an examination of the hospital's books, that there was no subject missing from the dissecting-room.'

'Who would be in charge of such bodies?'

'William Watts, the dissecting-room attendant.'

'Is William Watts present?' inquired the Coroner of the officer.

William Watts was present and could be called if the Coroner thought it necessary.

'I suppose no dead body would be delivered to the hospital without your knowledge, Sir Julian?'

'Certainly not.'

'Thank you. Will you proceed with your statement?'

'Inspector Sugg then asked me whether I

would send a medical man round to view the body. I said that I would go myself.'

'Why did you do that?'

'I confess to my share of ordinary human curiosity, Mr Coroner.'

Laughter from a medical student at the back of the court.

'On arriving at the flat I found the deceased lying on his back in the bath. I examined him, and came to the conclusion that death had been caused by a blow on the back of the neck dislocating the fourth and fifth cervical vertebrae, bruising the spinal cord and producing internal haemorrhage and partial paralysis of the brain. I judged the deceased to have been dead at least twelve hours, possibly more. I observed no other sign of violence of any kind upon the body. Deceased was a strong, well-nourished man of about fifty to fifty-five years of age.'

'In your opinion, could the blow have been self-inflicted?'

'Certainly not. It had been made with a heavy, blunt instrument from behind, with great force and considerable judgement. It is quite impossible that it was self-inflicted.'

'Could it have been the result of an accident?'

'That is possible, of course.'

'If, for example, the deceased had been looking out of the window, and the sash had shut violently down upon him?'

'No; in that case there would have been signs of strangulation and a bruise upon the throat as well.'

'But deceased might have been killed through

a heavy weight accidentally falling upon him?'

'He might.'

'Was death instantaneous, in your opinion?'

'It is difficult to say. Such a blow might very well cause death instantaneously, or the patient might linger in a partially paralysed condition for some time. In the present case I should be disposed to think that deceased might have lingered for some hours. I base my decision upon the condition of the brain revealed at the autopsy. I may say, however, that Dr Grimbold and I are not in complete agreement on the point.'

'I understand that a suggestion has been made as to the identification of the deceased. You are not in a position to identify him?'

'Certainly not. I never saw him before. The suggestion to which you refer is a preposterous one, and ought never to have been made. I was not aware until this morning that it had been made; had it been made to me earlier, I should have known how to deal with it, and I should like to express my strong disapproval of the unnecessary shock and distress inflicted upon a lady with whom I have the honour to be acquainted.'

The Coroner: 'It was not my fault, Sir Julian; I had nothing to do with it; I agree with you that it was unfortunate you were not consulted.'

The reporters scribbled busily, and the court asked each other what was meant, while the jury tried to look as if they knew already.

'In the matter of the eyeglasses found upon the body, Sir Julian. Do these give any indication to a medical man?'

'They were somewhat unusual lenses; an oculist would be able to speak more definitely, but I will say for myself that I should have expected them to belong to an older man than the deceased.'

'Speaking as a physician, who has had many opportunities of observing the human body, did you gather anything from the appearance of the deceased as to his personal habits?'

'I should say that he was a man in easy circumstances, but who had only recently come into money. His teeth are in a bad state, and his hands show signs of recent manual labour.'

'An Australian colonist, for instance, who had made money?'

'Something of that sort; of course, I could not say positively.'

'Of course not. Thank you, Sir Julian.'

Dr Grimbold, called, corroborated his distinguished colleague in every particular, except that, in his opinion, death had not occurred for several days after the blow. It was with the greatest hesitancy that he ventured to differ from Sir Julian Freke, and he might be wrong. It was difficult to tell in any case, and when he saw the body, deceased had been dead at least twenty-four hours, in his opinion.

Inspector Sugg, recalled. Would he tell the jury what steps had been taken to identify the deceased?

A description had been sent to every police station and had been inserted in all the newspapers. In view of the suggestion made by Sir Julian Freke, had inquiries been made at all the seaports? They had. And with no results? With no results at all. No one had come forward to identify the body? Plenty of people had come forward; but nobody succeeded in identifying it. Had any effort been made to follow up the clue afforded by the eye-glasses? Inspector Sugg submitted that, having regard to the interests of justice, he would beg to be excused from answering that question. Might the jury see the eye-glasses? The eyeglasses were handed to the jury.

William Watts, called, confirmed the evidence of Sir Julian Freke with regard to dissecting-room subjects. He explained the system by which they were entered. They usually were supplied by the workhouses and free hospitals. They were under his sole charge. The young gentlemen could not possibly get the keys. Had Sir Julian Freke, or any of the house surgeons, the keys? No, not even Sir Julian Freke. The keys had remained in his possession on Monday night? They had. And, in any case, the inquiry was irrelevant, as there was no body missing, nor ever had been? That was the case.

The Coroner then addressed the jury, reminding them with some asperity that they were not there to gossip about who the deceased could or could not have been, but to give their opinion as to the cause of death. He reminded them that they should consider whether, according to the medical evidence, death could have been accidental or self-inflicted, or whether it was deliberate murder, or homicide. If they considered the evidence on this point insufficient, they could return an open verdict. In any case, their verdict could not prejudice any person; if they brought it in 'murder', all the whole evidence would have to be gone through again before the magistrate. He then dismissed them, with the unspoken adjuration to be quick about it.

Sir Julian Freke, after giving his evidence, had caught the eye of the Duchess, and now came over and greeted her.

'I haven't seen you for an age,' said that lady. 'How are you?'

'Hard at work,' said the specialist. 'Just got my new book out. This kind of thing wastes time. Have you seen Lady Levy yet?'

'No, poor dear,' said the Duchess. 'I only came up this morning, for this. Mrs Thipps is staying with me — one of Peter's eccentricities, you know. Poor Christine! I must run round and see her. This is Mr Parker,' she added, 'who is investigating that case.'

'Oh,' said Sir Julian, and paused. 'Do you know,' he said in a low voice to Parker, 'I am very glad to meet you. Have you seen Lady Levy yet?'

'I saw her this morning.'

'Did she ask you to go on with the inquiry?'

'Yes,' said Parker; 'she thinks,' he added, 'that Sir Reuben may be detained in the hands of some financial rival or that perhaps some scoundrels are holding him to ransom.'

'And is that *your* opinion?' asked Sir Julian.

'I think it very likely,' said Parker, frankly.

Sir Julian hesitated again.

'I wish you would walk back with me when

this is over,' he said.

'I should be delighted,' said Parker.

At this moment the jury returned and took their places, and there was a little rustle and hush. The Coroner addressed the foreman and inquired if they were agreed upon their verdict.

'We are agreed, Mr Coroner, that deceased died of the effects of a blow upon the spine, but how that injury was inflicted we consider that there is not sufficient evidence to show.'

★   ★   ★

Mr Parker and Sir Julian Freke walked up the road together.

'I had absolutely no idea until I saw Lady Levy this morning,' said the doctor, 'that there was any idea of connecting this matter with the disappearance of Sir Reuben. The suggestion was perfectly monstrous, and could only have grown up in the mind of that ridiculous police officer. If I had had any idea what was in his mind I could have disabused him and avoided all this.'

'I did my best to do so,' said Parker, 'as soon as I was called in to the Levy case — '

'Who called you in, if I may ask?' inquired Sir Julian.

'Well, the household first of all, and then Sir Reuben's uncle, Mr Levy of Portman Square, wrote to me to go on with the investigation.'

'And now Lady Levy has confirmed those instructions?'

'Certainly,' said Parker in some surprise.

Sir Julian was silent for a little time.

'I'm afraid I was the first person to put the idea into Sugg's head,' said Parker, rather penitently. 'When Sir Reuben disappeared, my first step, almost, was to hunt up all the street accidents and suicides and so on that had turned up during the day, and I went down to see this Battersea Park body as a matter of routine. Of course, I saw that the thing was ridiculous as soon as I got there, but Sugg froze on to the idea — and it's true there was a good deal of resemblance between the dead man and the portraits I've seen of Sir Reuben.'

'A strong superficial likeness,' said Sir Julian. 'The upper part of the face is a not uncommon type, and as Sir Reuben wore a heavy beard and there was no opportunity of comparing the mouths and chins, I can understand the idea occurring to anybody. But only to be dismissed at once. I am sorry,' he added, 'as the whole matter has been painful to Lady Levy. You may know, Mr Parker, that I am an old, though I should not call myself an intimate, friend of the Levys.'

'I understood something of the sort.'

'Yes. When I was a young man I — in short, Mr Parker, I hoped once to marry Lady Levy.' (Mr Parker gave the usual sympathetic groan.) 'I have never married, as you know,' pursued Sir Julian. 'We have remained good friends. I have always done what I could to spare her pain.'

'Believe me, Sir Julian,' said Parker, 'that I sympathise very much with you and with Lady Levy, and that I did all I could to disabuse Inspector Sugg of this notion. Unhappily, the coincidence of Sir Reuben's being seen that evening in the Battersea Park Road — '

'Ah, yes,' said Sir Julian. 'Dear me, here we are at home. Perhaps you would come in for a moment, Mr Parker, and have tea or a whisky-and-soda or something.'

Parker promptly accepted this invitation, feeling that there were other things to be said.

The two men stepped into a square, finely furnished hall with a fireplace on the same side as the door, and a staircase opposite. The dining-room door stood open on their right, and as Sir Julian rang the bell a man-servant appeared at the far end of the hall.

'What will you take?' asked the doctor.

'After that dreadfully cold place,' said Parker, 'what I really want is gallons of hot tea, if you, as a nerve specialist, can bear the thought of it.'

'Provided you allow of a judicious blend of China in it,' replied Sir Julian in the same tone, 'I have no objection to make. Tea in the library at once,' he added to the servant, and led the way upstairs.

'I don't use the downstairs rooms much, except the dining-room,' he explained as he ushered his guest into a small but cheerful library on the first floor. 'This room leads out of my bedroom and is more convenient. I only live part of my time here, but it's very handy for my research work at the hospital. That's what I do there, mostly. It's a fatal thing for a theorist, Mr Parker, to let the practical work get behindhand. Dissection is the basis of all good theory and all correct diagnosis. One must keep one's hand and eye in training. This place is far more important to me than Harley Street, and some day I shall abandon my consulting practice altogether and settle down here to cut up my subjects and write my books in peace. So many things in this life are a waste of time, Mr Parker.'

Mr Parker assented to this.

'Very often,' said Sir Julian, 'the only time I get for any research work — necessitating as it does the keenest observation and the faculties at their acutest — has to be at night, after a long day's work and by artificial light, which, magnificent as the lighting of the dissecting-room here is, is always more trying to the eyes than daylight. Doubtless your own work has to be carried on under even more trying conditions.'

'Yes, sometimes,' said Parker; 'but then you see,' he added, 'the conditions are, so to speak, part of the work.'

'Quite so, quite so,' said Sir Julian; 'you mean that the burglar, for example, does not demonstrate his methods in the light of day, or plant the perfect footmark in the middle of a damp patch of sand for you to analyse.'

'Not as a rule,' said the detective, 'but I have no doubt many of your diseases work quite as insidiously as any burglar.'

'They do, they do,' said Sir Julian, laughing, 'and it is my pride, as it is yours, to track them down for the good of society. The neuroses, you know, are particularly clever criminals — they break out into as many disguises as — '

'As Leon Kestrel, the Master-Mummer,' suggested Parker, who read railway-stall detective stories on the principle of the busman's holiday.

'No doubt,' said Sir Julian, who did not, 'and they cover up their tracks wonderfully. But when you can really investigate, Mr Parker, and break up the dead, or for preference the living body with the scalpel, you always find the footmarks — the little trail of ruin or disorder left by madness or disease or drink or any other similar pest. But the difficulty is to trace them back, merely by observing the surface symptoms — the hysteria, crime, religion, fear, shyness, conscience, or whatever it may be; just as you observe a theft or a murder and look for the footsteps of the criminal, so I observe a fit of hysterics or an outburst of piety and hunt for the little mechanical irritation which has produced it.'

'You regard all these things as physical?'

'Undoubtedly. I am not ignorant of the rise of another school of thought, Mr Parker, but its exponents are mostly charlatans or self-deceivers. *'Sie haben sich so weit darin eingeheimnisst'* that, like sludge the Medium, they are beginning to believe their own nonsense, I should like to have the exploring of some of their brains, Mr Parker; I would show you the little faults and landslips in the cells — the misfiring and short-circuiting of the nerves, which produce these notions and these books. At least,' he added, gazing sombrely at his guest, 'at least, if I could not quite show you today, I shall be able to do so tomorrow — or in a year's time — or before I die.'

He sat for some minutes gazing into the fire,

while the red light played upon his tawny beard and struck out answering gleams from his compelling eyes.

Parker drank tea in silence, watching him. On the whole, however, he remained but little interested in the causes of nervous phenomena and his mind strayed to Lord Peter, coping with the redoubtable Crimplesham down in Salisbury. Lord Peter had wanted him to come; that meant, either that Crimplesham was proving recalcitrant or that a clue wanted following. But Bunter had said that tomorrow would do, and it was just as well. After all, the Battersea affair was not Parker's case; he had already wasted valuable time attending an inconclusive inquest, and he really ought to get on with his legitimate work. There was still Levy's secretary to see and the little matter of the Peruvian Oil to be looked into. He looked at his watch.

'I am very much afraid — if you will excuse me — ' he murmured.

Sir Julian came back with a start to the consideration of actuality.

'Your work calls you?' he said, smiling. 'Well, I can understand that. I won't keep you. But I wanted to say something to you in connection with your present inquiry — only I hardly know — I hardly like — '

Parker sat down again, and banished every indication of hurry from his face and attitude.

'I shall be very grateful for any help you can give me,' he said.

'I'm afraid it's more in the nature of hindrance,' said Sir Julian, with a short laugh.

'It's a case of destroying a clue for you, and a breach of professional confidence on my side. But since — accidentally — a certain amount has come out, perhaps the whole had better do so.'

Mr Parker made the encouraging noise which, among laymen, supplies the place of the priest's insinuating 'Yes, my son?'

'Sir Reuben Levy's visit on Monday night was to me,' said Sir Julian.

'Yes?' said Mr Parker, without expression.

'He found cause for certain grave suspicions concerning his health,' said Sir Julian, slowly, as though weighing how much he could in honour disclose to a stranger. 'He came to me, in preference to his own medical man, as he was particularly anxious that the matter should be kept from his wife. As I told you, he knew me fairly well, and Lady Levy had consulted me about a nervous disorder in the summer.'

'Did he make an appointment with you?' asked Parker.

'I beg your pardon,' said the other, absently.

'Did he make an appointment?'

'An appointment? Oh, no. He turned up suddenly in the evening after dinner when I wasn't expecting him. I took him up here and examined him, and he left me somewhere about ten o'clock, I should think.'

'May I ask what was the result of your examination?'

'Why do you want to know?'

'It might illuminate — well, conjecture as to his subsequent conduct,' said Parker, cautiously.

This story seemed to have little coherence with the rest of the business, and he wondered whether coincidence was alone responsible for Sir Reuben's disappearance on the same night that he visited the doctor.

'I see,' said Sir Julian. 'Yes. Well, I will tell you in confidence that I saw grave grounds of suspicion, but as yet, no absolute certainty of mischief.'

'Thank you. Sir Reuben left you at ten o'clock?'

'Then or thereabouts. I did not at first mention the matter as it was so very much Sir Reuben's wish to keep his visit to me secret, and there was no question of accident in the street or anything of that kind, since he reached home safely at midnight.'

'Quite so,' said Parker.

'It would have been, and is, a breach of confidence,' said Sir Julian, 'and I only tell you now because Sir Reuben was accidentally seen, and because I would rather tell you in private than have you ferreting round here and questioning my servants, Mr Parker. You will excuse my frankness.'

'Certainly,' said Parker. 'I hold no brief for the pleasantness of my profession, Sir Julian. I am very much obliged to you for telling me this. I might otherwise have wasted valuable time following up a false trail.'

'I am sure I need not ask you, in your turn, to respect this confidence,' said the doctor. 'To publish the matter abroad could only harm Sir Reuben and pain his wife, besides placing me in no favourable light with my patients.'

'I promise to keep the thing to myself,' said Parker, 'except of course,' he added hastily, 'that I must inform my colleague.'

'You have a colleague in the case?'

'I have.'

'What sort of person is he?'

'He will be perfectly discreet, Sir Julian.'

'Is he a police officer?'

'You need not be afraid of your confidence getting into the records at Scotland Yard.'

'I see that you know how to be discreet, Mr Parker.'

'We also have our professional etiquette, Sir Julian.'

★   ★   ★

On returning to Great Ormond Street, Mr Parker found a wire awaiting him, which said: 'Do not trouble to come. All well. Returning tomorrow. Wimsey.'

7

On returning to the flat just before lunchtime on the following morning, after a few confirmatory researches in Balham and the neighbourhood of Victoria Station, Lord Peter was greeted at the door by Mr Bunter (who had gone straight home from Waterloo), with a telephone message and a severe and nursemaidlike eye.

'Lady Swaffham rang me up, my lord, and said she hoped your lordship had not forgotten you were lunching with her.'

'I have forgotten, Bunter, and I mean to forget, I trust you told her I had succumbed to lethargic encephalitis suddenly, no flowers by request.'

'Lady Swaffham said, my lord, she was counting on you. She met the Duchess of Denver yesterday — '

'If my sister-in-law's there I won't go, that's flat,' said Lord Peter.

'I beg your pardon, my lord, the Dowager Duchess.'

'What's she doing in town?'

'I imagine she came up for the inquest, my lord.'

'Oh yes — we missed that, Bunter.'

'Yes, my lord. Her Grace is lunching with Lady Swaffham.'

'Bunter, I can't. I can't, really. Say I'm in bed with whooping cough, and ask my mother to come round after lunch.'

'Very well, my lord, Mrs Tommy Frayle will be at Lady Swaffham's, my lord, and Mr Milligan — '

'Mr Who?'

'Mr John P. Milligan, my lord, and — '

'Good God, Bunter, why didn't you say so before? Have I time to get there before he does? All right. I'm off. With a taxi I can just — '

'Not in those trousers, my lord,' said Mr Bunter, blocking the way to the door with deferential firmness.

'Oh, Bunter,' pleaded his lordship, 'do let me — just this once. You don't know how important it is.'

'Not on any account, my lord. It would be as much as my place is worth.'

'The trousers are all right, Bunter.'

'Not for Lady Swaffham's, my lord. Besides, your lordship forgets the man that ran against you with a milk-can at Salisbury.'

And Mr Bunter laid an accusing finger on a slight stain of grease showing across the light cloth.

'I wish to God I'd never let you grow into a privileged family retainer, Bunter,' said Lord Peter, bitterly, dashing his walking-stick into the umbrella stand. 'You've no conception of the mistakes my mother may be making.'

Mr Bunter smiled grimly and led his victim away.

When an immaculate Lord Peter was ushered, rather late for lunch, into Lady Swaffham's drawing-room the Dowager Duchess of Denver was seated on a sofa, plunged in intimate conversation with Mr John P. Milligan of Chicago.

★   ★   ★

'I'm vurry pleased to meet you, Duchess,' had been that financier's opening remark, 'to thank you for your exceedingly kind invitation. I assure you it's a compliment I deeply appreciate.'

The Duchess beamed at him, while conducting a rapid rally of all her intellectual forces.

'Do come and sit down and talk to me, Mr Milligan,' she said. 'I do so love talking to you great business men — let me see, is it a railway king you are or something about puss-in-the-corner — at least, I don't mean that exactly, but that game one used to play with cards, all about wheat and oats, and there was a bull and a bear, too — or was it a horse? — no, a bear, because I remember one always had to try and get rid of it and it used to get so dreadfully crumpled and torn, poor thing, always being handed about, one got to recognise it, and then one had to buy a new pack — so foolish it must seem to you, knowing the real thing, and dreadfully noisy, but really excellent for breaking the ice with rather stiff people who didn't know each other — I'm quite sorry it's gone out.'

Mr Milligan sat down.

'Wal, now,' he said, 'I guess it's as interesting for us business men to meet British aristocrats as it is for Britishers to meet American railway kings, Duchess. And I guess I'll make as many mistakes talking your kind of talk as you would make if you were tryin' to run a corner of wheat in Chicago. Fancy now, I called that fine lad of yours Lord Wimsey the other day, and he thought I'd mistaken him for his brother. That made me feel rather green.'

This was an unhoped-for lead. The Duchess walked warily.

'Dear boy,' she said, 'I am so glad you met him, Mr Milligan. *Both* my sons are a *great* comfort to me, you know, though, of course, Gerald is more conventional — but the right kind of person for the House of Lords, you know, and a splendid farmer. I can't see Peter down at Denver half so well, though he is always going to all the right things in town, and very amusing sometimes, poor boy.'

'I was vurry much gratified by Lord Peter's suggestion,' pursued Mr Milligan, 'for which I understand you are responsible, and I'll surely be very pleased to come any day you like, though I think you're flattering me too much.'

'Ah, well,' said the Duchess, 'I don't know if you're the best judge of that, Mr Milligan. Not that I know anything about business myself,' she added. 'I'm rather old-fashioned for these days, you know, and I can't pretend to do more than know a nice *man* when I see him; for the other things I rely on my son.'

The accent of this speech was so flattering that Mr Milligan purred almost audibly, and said:

'Wal, Duchess, I guess that's where a lady with a real, beautiful, old-fashioned soul has the advantage of these modern young blatherskites

— there aren't many men who wouldn't be nice — to her, and even then, if they aren't rock-bottom she can see through them.'

'But that leaves me where I was,' thought the Duchess. 'I believe,' she said aloud, 'that I ought to be thanking you in the name of the vicar of Duke's Denver for a very munificent cheque which reached him yesterday for the Church Restoration Fund. He was so delighted and astonished, poor dear man.'

'Oh, that's nothing,' said Mr Milligan, 'we haven't any fine old crusted buildings like yours over on our side, so it's a privilege to be allowed to drop a little kerosene into the worm-holes when we hear of one in the old country suffering from senile decay. So when your lad told me about Duke's Denver I took the liberty to subscribe without waiting for the Bazaar.'

'I'm sure it was very kind of you,' said the Duchess. 'You are coming to the Bazaar, then?' she continued, gazing into his face appealingly.

'Sure thing,' said Mr Milligan, with great promptness. 'Lord Peter said you'd let me know for sure about the date, but we can always make time for a little bit of good work anyway. Of course I'm hoping to be able to avail myself of your kind invitation to stop, but if I'm rushed, I'll manage anyhow to pop over and speak my piece and pop back again.'

'I hope so very much,' said the Duchess. 'I must see what can be done about the date — of course, I can't promise — '

'No, no,' said Mr Milligan heartily. 'I know what these things are to fix up. And then there's not only me — there's all the real big men of European eminence your son mentioned, to be consulted.'

The Duchess turned pale at the thought that any one of these illustrious persons might some time turn up in somebody's drawing-room, but by this time she had dug herself in comfortably, and was even beginning to find her range.

'I can't say how grateful we are to you,' she said, 'it will be such a treat. Do tell me what you think of saying.'

'Wal — ' began Mr Milligan.

Suddenly everybody was standing up and a penitent voice was heard to say:

'Really, most awfully sorry, y'know — hope you'll forgive me, Lady Swaffham, what? Dear lady, could I possibly forget an invitation from you? Fact is, I had to go an' see a man down in Salisbury — absolutely true, 'pon my word, and the fellow wouldn't let me get away. I'm simply grovellin' before you, Lady Swaffham. Shall I go an' eat my lunch in the corner?'

Lady Swaffham gracefully forgave the culprit.

'Your dear mother is here,' she said.

'How do, Mother?' said Lord Peter uneasily.

'How are you, dear?' replied the Duchess. 'You really oughtn't to have turned up just yet. Mr Milligan was just going to tell me what a thrilling speech he's preparing for the Bazaar, when you came and interrupted us.'

Conversation at lunch turned, not unnaturally, on the Battersea inquest, the Duchess giving a vivid impersonation of Mrs Thipps being interrogated by the Coroner.

' 'Did you hear anything unusual in the night?' says the little man, leaning forward and screaming at her, and so crimson in the face and his ears sticking out so — just like a cherubim in that poem of Tennyson's — or is a cherub blue? — perhaps it's seraphim I mean — anyway you know what I mean, all eyes, with little wings on its head. And dear old Mrs Thipps saying, 'Of course I have, any time these eighty years', and *such* a sensation in court till they found out she thought he'd said, 'Do you sleep without a light?' and everybody laughing, and then the Coroner said quite loudly, 'Damn the woman', and she heard that, I can't think why, and said: 'Don't you get swearing, young man, sitting there in the presence of Providence, as you may say, I don't know what young people are coming to nowadays' — and he's sixty if he's a day, you know,' said the Duchess. By a natural transition, Mrs Tommy Frayle referred to the man who was hanged for murdering three brides in a bath.

'I always thought that was so ingenious,' she said, gazing soulfully at Lord Peter, 'and do you know, as it happened, Tommy had just made me insure my life, and I got so frightened, I gave up my morning bath and took to having it in the afternoon when he was in the House — I mean, when he was *not* in the house — not at home, I mean.'

'Dear lady,' said Lord Peter, reproachfully, 'I have a distinct recollection that all those brides were thoroughly unattractive. But it was an

140

uncommonly ingenious plan — the first time of askin' — only he shouldn't have repeated himself.'

'One demands a little more originality in these days, even from murderers,' said Lady Swaffham. 'Like dramatists, you know — so much easier in Shakespeare's time, wasn't it? Always the same girl dressed up as a man, and even that borrowed from Boccaccio or Dante or somebody. I'm sure if I'd been a Shakespeare hero, the very minute I saw a slim-legged young page-boy I'd have said: 'Odsbodikins! There's that girl again!''

'That's just what happened, as a matter of fact,' said Lord Peter. 'You see, Lady Swaffham, if ever you want to commit a murder, the thing you've got to do is to prevent people from associatin' their ideas. Most people don't associate anythin' — their ideas just roll about like so many dry peas on a tray, makin' a lot of noise an' goin' nowhere, but once you begin lettin' 'em string their peas into a necklace, it's goin' to be strong enough to hang you, what?'

'Dear me!' said Mrs Tommy Frayle, with a little scream, 'what a blessing it is none of my friends have any ideas at all!'

'Y'see,' said Lord Peter, balancing a piece of duck on his fork and frowning, 'it's only in Sherlock Holmes and stories like that, that people think things out logically. Or'nar'ly, if somebody tells you somethin' out of the way, you just say, 'By Jove!' or 'How sad!' an' leave it at that, an' half the time you forget about it, 'nless somethin' turns up afterwards to drive it

141

home. F'r instance, Lady Swaffham, I told you when I came in that I'd been down to Salisbury, 'n' that's true, only I don't suppose it impressed you much; 'n' I don't suppose it'd impress you much if you read in the paper tomorrow of a tragic discovery of a dead lawyer down in Salisbury, but if I went to Salisbury again next week 'n' there was a Salisbury doctor found dead the day after, you might begin to think I was a bird of ill omen for Salisbury residents; and if I went there again the week after, 'n' you heard next day that the see of Salisbury had fallen vacant suddenly, you might begin to wonder what took me to Salisbury, an' why I'd never mentioned before that I had friends down there, don't you see, an' you might think of goin' down to Salisbury yourself an' askin' all kinds of people if they'd happened to see a young man in plum-coloured socks hangin' round the Bishop's Palace.'

'I daresay I should,' said Lady Swaffham.

'Quite. An' if you found that the lawyer and the doctor had once upon a time been in business at Poggleton-on-the-Marsh when the bishop had been vicar there, you'd begin to remember you'd once heard of me payin' a visit to Poggleton-on-the-Marsh a long time ago, an' you'd begin to look up the parish registers there an' discover I'd been married under an assumed name by the vicar to the widow of a wealthy farmer, who'd died suddenly of peritonitis, as certified by the doctor, after the lawyer'd made a will leavin' me all her money, and *then* you'd begin to think I might have very good reasons for gettin' rid of such promisin' blackmailers as the lawyer, the doctor an' the bishop. Only, if I hadn't started an association in your mind by gettin' rid of 'em all in the same place, you'd never have thought of goin' to Poggleton-on-the-Marsh, 'n' you wouldn't even have remembered I'd ever been there.'

'Were you ever there, Lord Peter?' inquired Mrs Tommy, anxiously.

'I don't think so,' said Lord Peter, 'the name threads no beads in my mind. But it might, any day, you know.'

'But if you were investigating a crime,' said Lady Swaffham, 'you'd have to begin by the usual things, I suppose — finding out what the person had been doing, and who'd been to call, and looking for a motive, wouldn't you?'

'Oh, yes,' said Lord Peter, 'but most of us have such dozens of motives for murderin' all sorts of inoffensive people. There's lots of people I'd like to murder, wouldn't you?'

'Heaps,' said Lady Swaffham. 'There's that dreadful — perhaps I'd better not say it, though, for fear you should remember it later on.'

'Well, I wouldn't if I were you,' said Peter, amiably. 'You never know. It'd be beastly awkward if the person died suddenly tomorrow.'

'The difficulty with this Battersea case, I guess,' said Mr Milligan, 'is that nobody seems to have any associations with the gentleman in the bath.'

'So hard on poor Inspector Sugg,' said the Duchess. 'I quite felt for the man, having to stand up there and answer a lot of questions when he had nothing at all to say.'

Lord Peter applied himself to the duck, having got a little behindhand. Presently he heard somebody ask the Duchess if she had seen Lady Levy.

'She is in great distress,' said the woman who had spoken, a Mrs Freemantle, 'though she clings to the hope that he will turn up. I suppose you knew him, Mr Milligan — know him, I should say, for I hope he's still alive somewhere.'

Mrs Freemantle was the wife of an eminent railway director, and celebrated for her ignorance of the world of finance. Her *faux pas* in this connection enlivened the tea parties of city men's wives.

'Wal, I've dined with him,' said Mr Milligan, good-naturedly. 'I think he and I've done our best to ruin each other, Mrs Freemantle. If this were the States,' he added, 'I'd be much inclined to suspect myself of having put Sir Reuben in a safe place. But we can't do business that way in your old country; no, ma'am.'

'It must be exciting work doing business in America,' said Lord Peter.

'It is,' said Mr Milligan. 'I guess my brothers are having a good time there now. I'll be joining them again before long, as soon as I've fixed up a little bit of work for them on this side.'

'Well, you mustn't go till after my bazaar,' said the Duchess.

★ ★ ★

Lord Peter spent the afternoon in a vain hunt for Mr Parker. He ran him down eventually after

144

dinner in Great Ormond Street.

Parker was sitting in an elderly but affectionate arm-chair, with his feet on the mantelpiece, relaxing his mind with a modern commentary on the Epistle to the Galatians. He received Lord Peter with quiet pleasure, though without rapturous enthusiasm, and mixed him a whisky-and-soda. Peter took up the book his friend had laid down and glanced over the pages.

'All these men work with a bias in their minds, one way or other,' he said; 'they find what they are looking for.'

'Oh, they do,' agreed the detective, 'but one learns to discount that almost automatically, you know. When I was at college, I was all on the other side — Conybeare and Robertson and Drews and those people, you know, till I found they were all so busy looking for a burglar whom nobody had ever seen, that they couldn't recognise the footprints of the household, so to speak. Then I spent two years learning to be cautious.'

'Hum,' said Lord Peter, 'theology must be good exercise for the brain then, for you're easily the most cautious devil I know. But I say, do go on reading — it's a shame for me to come and root you up in your off-time like this.'

'It's all right, old man,' said Parker.

The two men sat silent for a little, and then Lord Peter said:

'D'you like your job?'

The detective considered the question, and replied:

'Yes — yes, I do. I know it to be useful, and I

am fitted to it. I do it quite well — not with inspiration, perhaps, but sufficiently well to take a pride in it. It is full of variety and it forces one to keep up to the mark and not get slack. And there's a future to it. Yes, I like it. Why?'

'Oh, nothing,' said Peter. 'It's a hobby to me, you see. I took it up when the bottom of things was rather knocked out for me, because it was so damned exciting, and the worst of it is, I enjoy it — up to a point. If it was all on paper I'd enjoy every bit of it. I love the beginning of a job — when one doesn't know any of the people and it's just exciting and amusing. But if it comes to really running down a live person and getting him hanged, or even quodded, poor devil, there don't seem as if there was any excuse for me buttin' in, since I don't have to make my livin' by it. And I feel as if I oughtn't ever to find it amusin'. But I do.'

Parker gave this speech his careful attention.

'I see what you mean,' he said.

'There's old Milligan, f'r instance,' said Lord Peter. 'On paper, nothin' would be funnier than to catch old Milligan out. But he's rather a decent old bird to talk to. Mother likes him. He's taken a fancy to me. It's awfully entertainin' goin' and pumpin' him with stuff about a bazaar for church expenses, but when he's so jolly pleased about it and that, I feel a worm. S'pose old Milligan has cut Levy's throat and plunged him into the Thames. It ain't my business.'

'It's as much yours as anybody's,' said Parker; 'it's no better to do it for money than to do it for nothing.'

146

'Yes, it is,' said Peter stubbornly. 'Havin' to live is the only excuse there is for doin' that kind of thing.'

'Well, but look here!' said Parker. 'If Milligan has cut poor old Levy's throat for no reason except to make himself richer, I don't see why he should buy himself off by giving £1,000 to Duke's Denver church roof, or why he should be forgiven just because he's childishly vain, or childishly snobbish.'

'That's a nasty one,' said Lord Peter.

'Well, if you like, even because he has taken a fancy to you.'

'No, but — '

'Look here, Wimsey — do you think he *has* murdered Levy?'

'Well, he may have.'

'But do you think he has?'

'I don't want to think so.'

'Because he has taken a fancy to you?'

'Well, that biases me, of course — '

'I daresay it's quite a legitimate bias. You don't think a callous murderer would be likely to take a fancy to you?'

'Well — besides, I've taken rather a fancy to him.'

'I daresay that's quite legitimate, too. You've observed him and made a subconscious deduction from your observations, and the result is, you don't think he did it. Well, why not? You're entitled to take that into account.'

'But perhaps I'm wrong, and he did do it.'

'Then why let your vainglorious conceit in your own power of estimating character stand in the way of unmasking the singularly cold-blooded murder of an innocent and lovable man?'

'I know — but I don't feel I'm playing the game somehow.'

'Look here, Peter,' said the other with some earnestness, 'suppose you get this playing-fields-of-Eton complex out of your system once and for all. There doesn't seem to be much doubt that something unpleasant has happened to Sir Reuben Levy. Call it murder, to strengthen the argument. If Sir Reuben has been murdered, is it a game? and is it fair to treat it as a game?'

'That's what I'm ashamed of, really,' said Lord Peter. 'It *is* a game to me, to begin with, and I go on cheerfully, and then I suddenly see that somebody is going to be hurt, and I want to get out of it.'

'Yes, yes, I know,' said the detective, 'but that's because you're thinking about your attitude. You want to be consistent, you want to look pretty, you want to swagger debonairly through a comedy of puppets or else to stalk magnificently through a tragedy of human sorrows and things. But that's childish. If you've any duty to society in the way of finding out the truth about murders, you must do it in any attitude that comes handy. You want to be elegant and detached? That's all right, if you find the truth out that way, but it hasn't any value in itself, you know. You want to look dignified and consistent — what's that got to do with it? You want to hunt down a murderer for the sport of the thing and then shake hands with him and say, 'Well played

— hard luck — you shall have your revenge tomorrow!' Well, you can't do it like that. Life's not a football match. You want to be a sportsman. You can't be a sportsman. You're a responsible person.'

'I don't think you ought to read so much theology,' said Lord Peter. 'It has a brutalising influence.'

He got up and paced about the room, looking idly over the bookshelves. Then he sat down again, filled and lit his pipe, and said:

'Well, I'd better tell you about the ferocious and hardened Crimplesham.'

He detailed his visit to Salisbury. Once assured of his *bona fides*, Mr Crimplesham had given him the fullest details of his visit to town.

'And I've substantiated it all,' groaned Lord Peter, 'and unless he's corrupted half Balham, there's no doubt he spent the night there. And the afternoon was really spent with the bank people. And half the residents of Salisbury seem to have seen him off on Monday before lunch. And nobody but his own family or young Wicks seems to have anything to gain by his death. And even if young Wicks wanted to make away with him, it's rather far-fetched to go and murder an unknown man in Thipps's place in order to stick Crimplesham's eyeglasses on his nose.'

'Where was young Wicks on Monday?' asked Parker.

'At a dance given by the Precentor,' said Lord Peter, wildly. 'David — his name is David — dancing before the ark of the Lord in the face of the whole Cathedral Close.'

There was a pause.

'Tell me about the inquest,' said Wimsey.

Parker obliged with a summary of the evidence.

'Do you believe the body could have been concealed in the flat after all?' he asked. 'I know we looked, but I suppose we might have missed something.'

'We might. But Sugg looked as well.'

'Sugg!'

'You do Sugg an injustice,' said Lord Peter; 'if there had been any signs of Thipps's complicity in the crime, Sugg would have found them.'

'Why?'

'Why? Because he was looking for them. He's like your commentators on Galatians. He thinks that either Thipps, or Gladys Horrocks, or Gladys Horrocks's young man did it. Therefore he found marks on the window-sill where Gladys Horrocks's young man might have come in or handed something in to Gladys Horrocks. He didn't find any signs on the roof, because he wasn't looking for them.'

'But he went over the roof before me.'

'Yes, but only in order to prove that there were no marks there. He reasons like this: Gladys Horrocks's young man is a glazier. Glaziers come on ladders. Glaziers have ready access to ladders. Therefore Gladys Horrocks's young man had ready access to a ladder. Therefore Gladys Horrocks's young man came on a ladder. Therefore there will be marks on the windowsill and none on the roof. Therefore he finds marks on the window-sill but none on the roof. He

150

finds no marks on the ground, but he thinks he would have found them if the yard didn't happen to be paved with asphalt. Similarly, he thinks Mr Thipps may have concealed the body in the box-room or elsewhere. Therefore you may be sure he searched the box-room and all the other places for signs of occupation. If they had been there he would have found them, because he was looking for them. Therefore, if he didn't find them it's because they weren't there.'

'All right,' said Parker, 'stop talking. I believe you.'

He went on to detail the medical evidence.

'By the way,' said Lord Peter, 'to skip across for a moment to the other case, has it occurred to you that perhaps Levy was going out to see Freke on Monday night?'

'He was; he did,' said Parker, rather unexpectedly, and proceeded to recount his interview with the nerve-specialist.

'Humph!' said Lord Peter. 'I say, Parker, these are funny cases, ain't they? Every line of inquiry seems to peter out. It's awfully exciting up to a point, you know, and then nothing comes of it. It's like rivers getting lost in the sand.'

'Yes,' said Parker. 'And there's another one I lost this morning.'

'What's that?'

'Oh, I was pumping Levy's secretary about his business. I couldn't get much that seemed important except further details about the Argentine and so on. Then I thought I'd just ask round in the City about those Peruvian Oil shares, but Levy hadn't even heard of them so far as I could make out. I routed out the brokers, and found a lot of mystery and concealment, as one always does, you know, when somebody's been rigging the market, and at least I found one name at the back of it. But it wasn't Levy's.'

'No? Whose was it?'

'Oddly enough, Freke's. It seems mysterious. He bought a lot of shares last week, in a secret kind of way, a few of them in his own name, and then quietly sold 'em out on Tuesday at a small profit — a few hundreds, not worth going to all that trouble about, you wouldn't think.'

'Shouldn't have thought he ever went in for that kind of gamble.'

'He doesn't as a rule. That's the funny part of it.'

'Well, you never know,' said Lord Peter; 'people do these things just to prove to themselves or somebody else that they could make a fortune that way if they liked. I've done it myself in a small way.'

He knocked out his pipe and rose to go.

'I say, old man,' he said suddenly, as Parker was letting him out, 'does it occur to you that Freke's story doesn't fit in awfully well with what Anderson said about the old boy having been so jolly at dinner on Monday night? Would you be, if you thought you'd got anything of that sort?'

'No, I shouldn't,' said Parker; 'but,' he added with his habitual caution, 'some men will jest in the dentist's waiting-room. You, for one.'

'Well, that's true,' said Lord Peter, and went downstairs.

8

Lord Peter reached home about midnight, feeling extraordinarily wakeful and alert. Something was jigging and worrying in his brain; it felt like a hive of bees, stirred up by a stick. He felt as though he were looking at a complicated riddle, of which he had once been told the answer but had forgotten it and was always on the point of remembering.

'Somewhere,' said Lord Peter to himself, 'somewhere I've got the key to these two things. I know I've got it, only I can't remember what it is. Somebody said it. Perhaps I said it. I can't remember where, but I know I've got it. Go to bed, Bunter, I shall sit up a little. I'll just slip on a dressing-gown.'

Before the fire he sat down with his pipe in his mouth and his jazz-coloured peacocks gathered about him. He traced out this line and that line of investigation — rivers running into the sand. They ran out from the thought of Levy, last seen at ten o'clock in Prince of Wales Road. They ran back from the picture of the grotesque dead man in Mr Thipps's bathroom — they ran over the roof, and were lost — lost in the sand. Rivers running into the sand — rivers running underground, very far down —

Where Alph, the sacred river, ran
Through caverns measureless to man

153

Down to a sunless sea.

By leaning his head down, it seemed to Lord Peter that he could hear them, very faintly, lipping and gurgling somewhere in the darkness. But where? He felt quite sure that somebody had told him once, only he had forgotten.

He roused himself, threw a log on the fire, and picked up a book which the indefatigable Bunter, carrying on his daily fatigues amid the excitements of special duty, had brought from the Times Book Club. It happened to be Sir Julian Freke's *Physiological Bases of the Conscience*, which he had seen reviewed two days before.

'This ought to send one to sleep,' said Lord Peter; 'if I can't leave these problems to my subconscious I'll be as limp as a rag tomorrow.'

He opened the book slowly, and glanced carelessly through the preface.

'I wonder if that's true about Levy being ill,' he though, putting the book down; 'it doesn't seem likely. And yet — Dash it all, I'll take my mind off it.'

He read on resolutely for a little.

'I don't suppose Mother's kept up with the Levys much,' was the next importunate train of thought. 'Dad always hated self-made people and wouldn't have 'em at Denver. And old Gerald keeps up the tradition. I wonder if she knew Freke well in those days. She seems to get on with Milligan. I trust Mother's judgement a good deal. She was a brick about that bazaar business. I ought to have warned her. She said something once — '

He pursued an elusive memory for some minutes, till it vanished altogether with a mocking flicker of the tail. He returned to his reading.

Presently another thought crossed his mind, aroused by a photograph of some experiment in surgery.

'If the evidence of Freke and that man Watts hadn't been so positive,' he said to himself, 'I should be inclined to look into the matter of those shreds of lint on the chimney.'

He considered this, shook his head, and read with determination.

Mind and matter were one thing, that was the theme of the physiologist. Matter could erupt, as it were, into ideas. You could carve passions in the brain with a knife. You could get rid of imagination with drugs and cure an outworn convention like a disease. 'The knowledge of good and evil is an observed phenomenon, attendant upon a certain condition of the brain cells, which is removable.' That was one phrase; and again:

'Conscience in man may, in fact, be compared to the sting of a hive-bee, which, so far from conducing to the welfare of its possessor, cannot function, even in a single instance, without occasioning its death. The survival-value in each case is thus purely social; and if humanity ever passes from its present phase of social development into that of a higher individualism, as some of our philosophers have ventured to speculate, we may suppose that this interesting mental phenomenon may gradually cease to appear; just as the nerves and muscles which once controlled the movements of our ears and scalps have, in all save a few backward individuals, become atrophied and of interest only to the physiologist.'

'By Jove!' thought Lord Peter, idly, 'that's an ideal doctrine for the criminal. A man who believed that would never — '

And then it happened — the thing he had been half-unconsciously expecting. It happened suddenly, surely, as unmistakably as sunrise. He remembered — not one thing, not another thing, nor a logical succession of things, but everything — the whole thing, perfect, complete, in all its dimensions as it were and instantaneously; as if he stood outside the world and saw it suspended in infinitely dimensional space. He no longer needed to reason about it, or even to think about it. He knew it.

There is a game in which one is presented with a jumble of letters and is required to make a word out of them, as thus:

COSSSSRI

The slow way of solving the problem is to try out all the permutations and combinations in turn, throwing away impossible conjunctions of letters, as:

SSSIRC
or
SCSRSO

Another way is to stare at the inco-ordinate elements until, by no logical process that the conscious mind can detect, or under some adventitious external stimulus, the combination

SCISSORS

presents itself with calm certainty. After that, one does not even need to arrange the letters in order. The thing is done.

Even so, the scattered elements of two grotesque conundrums, flung higgledy-piggledy into Lord Peter's mind, resolved themselves, unquestioned henceforward. A bump on the roof of the end house — Levy in a welter of cold rain talking to a prostitute in the Battersea Park Road — a single ruddy hair — lint bandages — Inspector Sugg calling the great surgeon from the dissecting-room of the hospital — Lady Levy with a nervous attack — the smell of carbolic soap — the Duchess's voice — 'not really an engagement, only a sort of understanding with her father' — shares in Peruvian Oil — the dark skin and curved, fleshy profile of the man in the bath — Dr Grimbold giving evidence, 'In my opinion, death did not occur for several days after the blow' — india-rubber gloves — even, even, faintly, the voice of Mr Appledore, 'He called on me, sir, with an anti-vivisectionist pamphlet' — all these things and many others rang together and made one sound, they swung together like bells in a steeple, with the deep tenor booming through the clamour:

'The knowledge of good and evil is a

phenomenon of the brain, and is removable, removable, removable. The knowledge of good and evil is removable.'

Lord Peter Wimsey was not a young man who habitually took himself very seriously, but this time he was frankly appalled. 'It's impossible,' said his reason, feebly; '*credo quia impossible*,' said his interior certainty with impervious self-satisfaction. 'All right,' said conscience, instantly allying itself with blind faith, 'what are you going to do about it?'

Lord Peter got up and paced the room: 'Good Lord!' he said. 'Good Lord!' He took down *Who's Who* from the little shelf over the telephone, and sought comfort in its pages.

FREKE, Sir Julian, Kt. cr. 1916; G.C.V.O. cr, 1919; K.C.V.O., 1917; K.C.B., 1918; M.D., F.R.C.P., F.R.C.S., Dr en Méd. Paris; D.Sci. Cantab.; Knight of Grace of the Order of S. John of Jerusalem; Consulting Surgeon of St Luke's Hospital, Battersea. *b.* Gryllingham, 16 March, 1872, *only son* of Edward Curzon Freke, Esq., of Gryll Court, Gryllingham. *Educ.* Harrow and Trinity Coll., Cambridge; Col. A.M.S.; late Member of the Advisory Board of the Army Medical Service. *Publications*: Some Notes on the Pathological Aspects of Genius, 1892; Statistical Contributions to the Study of Infantile Paralysis in England and Wales, 1894; Functional Disturbances of the Nervous System, 1899; Cerebro-Spinal Diseases, 1904; The Borderland of Insanity, 1906; An Examination into the Treatment of Pauper Lunacy in the

United Kingdom, 1906; Modern Developments in Psycho-Therapy: A Criticism, 1910; Criminal Lunacy, 1914; The Application of Psycho-Therapy to the Treatment of Shell-Shock, 1917; An Answer to Professor Freud, with a Description of Some Experiments Carried Out at the Base Hospital at Amiens, 1919; Structural Modifications Accompanying the More Important Neuroses, 1920. *Clubs*: White's; Oxford and Cambridge; Alpine, etc. *Recreations*: Chess, Mountaineering, Fishing. *Address*: 282 Harley Street and St Luke's House, Prince of Wales Road, Battersea Park, S.W.11.

He flung the book away. 'Confirmation!' he groaned. 'As if I needed it!'

He sat down again and buried his face in his hands. He remembered quite suddenly how, years ago, he had stood before the breakfast table at Denver Castle — a small, peaky boy in blue knickers, with a thunderously beating heart. The family had not come down; there was a great silver urn with a spirit lamp under it, and an elaborate coffee-pot boiling in a glass dome. He had twitched the corner of the tablecloth — twitched it harder, and the urn moved ponderously forward and all the teaspoons rattled. He seized the tablecloth in a firm grip and pulled his hardest — he could feel now the delicate and awful thrill as the urn and the coffee machine and the whole of a Sèvres breakfast service had crashed down in one stupendous ruin — he remembered the horrified face of the butler, and the screams of a lady guest.

A log broke across and sank into a fluff of white ash. A belated motor-lorry rumbled past the window.

Mr Bunter, sleeping the sleep of the true and faithful servant, was aroused in the small hours by a hoarse whisper, 'Bunter!'

'Yes, my lord,' said Bunter, sitting up and switching on the light.

'Put that light out, damn you!' said the voice. 'Listen — over there — listen — can't you hear it?'

'It's nothing, my lord,' said Mr Bunter, hastily getting out of bed and catching hold of his master; 'it's all right, you get to bed quick and I'll fetch you a drop of bromide. Why, you're all shivering — you've been sitting up too late.'

'Hush! no, no — it's the water,' said Lord Peter, with chattering teeth; 'it's up to their waists down there, poor devils. But listen! can't you hear it? Tap, tap, tap — they're mining us — but I don't know where — I can't hear — I can't. Listen, you! There it is again — we must find it — we must stop it . . . Listen! Oh, my God! I can't hear — I can't hear anything for the noise of the guns. Can't they stop the guns?'

'Oh dear!' said Mr Bunter to himself. 'No, no — it's all right, Major — don't you worry.'

'But I hear it,' protested Peter.

'So do I,' said Mr Bunter stoutly; 'very good hearing, too, my lord. That's our own sappers at work in the communication trench. Don't you fret about that, sir.'

Lord Peter grasped his wrist with a feverish hand.

'Our own sappers,' he said; 'sure of that?'

'Certain of it,' said Mr Bunter, cheerfully.

'They'll bring down the tower,' said Lord Peter.

'To be sure they will,' said Mr Bunter, 'and very nice, too. You just come and lay down a bit, sir — they're come to take over this section.'

'You're sure it's safe to leave it?' said Lord Peter.

'Safe as houses, sir,' said Mr Bunter, tucking his master's arm under his and walking him off to his bedroom.

Lord Peter allowed himself to be closed and put to bed without further resistance. Mr Bunter, looking singularly un-Bunterlike in striped pyjamas, with his stiff black hair ruffled about his head, sat grimly watching the younger man's sharp cheekbones and the purple stains under his eyes.

'Thought we'd had the last of these attacks,' he said. 'Been overdoin' of himself. Asleep?' He peered at him anxiously. An affectionate note crept into his voice. 'Bloody little fool!' said Sergeant Bunter.

9

Mr Parker, summoned the next morning to 110A Piccadilly, arrived to find the Dowager Duchess in possession. She greeted him charmingly.

'I am going to take this silly boy down to Denver for the week-end,' she said, indicating Peter, who was writing and only acknowledged his friend's entrance with a brief nod. 'He's been doing too much — running about to Salisbury and places and up till all hours of the night — you really shouldn't encourage him, Mr Parker, it's very naughty of you — waking poor Bunter up in the middle of the night with scares about Germans, as if that wasn't all over years ago, and he hasn't had an attack for ages, but there! Nerves are such funny things, and Peter always did have nightmares when he was quite a little boy — though very often of course it was only a little pill he wanted; but he was so dreadfully bad in 1918, you know, and I suppose we can't expect to forget all about a great war in a year or two, and, really, I ought to be very thankful with both my boys safe. Still, I think a little peace and quiet at Denver won't do him any harm.'

'Sorry you've been having a bad turn, old man,' said Parker, vaguely sympathetic; 'you're looking a bit seedy.'

'Charles,' said Lord Peter, in a voice entirely

162

void of expression, 'I am going away for a couple of days because I can be no use to you in London. What has got to be done for the moment can be much better done by you than by me. I want you to take this' — he folded up his writing and placed it in an envelope — 'to Scotland Yard immediately and get it sent out to all the work-houses, infirmaries, police stations, Y.M.C.A.s and so on in London. It is a description of Thipps's corpse as he was before he was shaved and cleaned up. I want to know whether any man answering to that description has been taken in anywhere, alive or dead, during the last fortnight. You will see Sir Andrew Mackenzie personally, and get the paper sent out at once, by his authority; you will tell him that you have solved the problems of the Levy murder and the Battersea mystery' — Mr Parker made an astonished noise to which his friend paid no attention — 'and you will ask him to have men in readiness with a warrant to arrest a very dangerous and important criminal at any moment on your information. When the replies to this paper come in, you will search for any mention of St Luke's Hospital, or of any person connected with St Luke's Hospital, and you will send for me at once.

'Meanwhile you will scrape acquaintance — I don't care how — with one of the students at St Luke's. Don't march in there blowing about murders and police warrants, or you may find yourself in Queer Street. I shall come up to town as soon as I hear from you, and I shall expect to find a nice ingenuous Sawbones here to meet

163

me.' He grinned faintly.

'D'you mean you've got to the bottom of this thing?' asked Parker.

'Yes. I may be wrong. I hope I am, but I know I'm not.'

'You won't tell me?'

'D'you know,' said Peter, 'honestly I'd rather not. I say I *may* be wrong — and I'd feel as if I'd libelled the Archbishop of Canterbury.'

'Well, tell me — is it one mystery or two?'

'One.'

'You talked of the Levy murder. Is Levy dead?'

'God — yes!' said Peter, with a strong shudder.

The Duchess looked up from where she was reading the *Tatler*.

'Peter,' she said, 'is that your ague coming on again? Whatever you two are chattering about, you'd better stop it at once if it excites you. Besides, it's about time to be off.'

'All right, Mother,' said Peter. He turned to Bunter, standing respectfully in the door with an overcoat and suitcase. 'You understand what you have to do, don't you?' he said.

'Perfectly, thank you, my lord. The car is just arriving, your Grace.'

'With Mrs Thipps inside it,' said the Duchess. 'She'll be delighted to see you again, Peter. You remind her so of Mr Thipps. Good morning, Bunter.'

'Good morning, your Grace.'

Parker accompanied them downstairs.

When they had gone he looked blankly at the paper in his hand — then, remembering that it

164

was Saturday and there was need for haste, he hailed a taxi.

'Scotland Yard!' he cried.

★ ★ ★

Tuesday morning saw Lord Peter and a man in a velveteen jacket swishing merrily through seven acres of turnip-tops, streaked yellow with early frosts. A little way ahead, a sinuous undercurrent of excitement among the leaves proclaimed the unseen yet ever-near presence of one of the Duke of Denver's setter pups. Presently a partridge flew up with a noise like a police rattle, and Lord Peter accounted for it very creditably for a man who, a few nights before, had been listening to imaginary German sappers. The setter bounded foolishly through the turnips, and fetched back the dead bird.

'Good dog,' said Lord Peter.

Encouraged by this, the dog gave a sudden ridiculous gambol and barked, its ear tossed inside out over its head.

'Heel,' said the man in velveteen, violently. The animal sidled up, ashamed.

'Fool of a dog, that,' said the man in velveteen: 'can't keep quiet. Too nervous, my lord. One of old Black Lass's pups.'

'Dear me,' said Peter, 'is the old dog still going?'

'No, my lord; we had to to put her away in the spring.'

Peter nodded. He always proclaimed that he hated the country, and was thankful to have

165

nothing to do with the family estates, but this morning he enjoyed the crisp air and the wet leaves washing darkly over his polished boots. At Denver things moved in an orderly way; no one died sudden and violent deaths except aged setters — and partridges, to be sure. He sniffed up the autumn smell with appreciation. There was a letter in his pocket which had come by the morning post, but he did not intend to read it just yet. Parker had not wired; there was no hurry.

⋆　⋆　⋆

He read it in the smoking-room after lunch. His brother was there, dozing over *The Times* — a good, clean Englishman, sturdy and conventional, rather like Henry VIII in his youth; Gerald, sixteenth Duke of Denver. The Duke considered his cadet rather degenerate, and not quite good form; he disliked his taste for police-court news.

The letter was from Mr Bunter.

110A Piccadilly,
W.1.

MY LORD:

I write (Mr Bunter had been carefully educated and knew that nothing is more vulgar than a careful avoidance of beginning a letter with the first person singular) as your lordship directed, to inform you of the result of my investigations.

I experienced no difficulty in becoming

acquainted with Sir Julian Freke's man-servant. He belongs to the same club as the Hon. Frederick Arbuthnot's man, who is a friend of mine, and was very willing to introduce me. He took me to the club yesterday (Sunday) evening, and we dined with the man, whose name is John Cummings, and afterwards I invited Cummings to drinks and a cigar in the flat. Your lordship will excuse me doing this, knowing that it is not my habit, but it has always been my experience that the best way to gain a man's confidence is to let him suppose that one takes advantage of one's employer.

('I always suspected Bunter of being a student of human nature,' commented Lord Peter.)

I gave him the best old port ('The deuce you did,' said Lord Peter), having heard you and Mr Arbuthnot talk over it. ('Hum!' said Lord Peter.)

Its effects were quite equal to my expectations as regards the principal matter in hand, but I very much regret to state that the man had so little understanding of what was offered to him that he smoked a cigar with it (one of your lordship's Villar y Villars). You will understand that I made no comment on this at the time, but your lordship will sympathise with my feelings. May I take this opportunity of expressing my grateful appreciation of your lordship's excellent taste in food, drink and dress? It is, if I may say so, more than a pleasure — it is an education, to valet and buttle your lordship.

Lord Peter bowed his head gravely.

'What on earth are you doing. Peter, sittin' there noddin' an' grinnin' like a what-you-may-call it?' demanded the Duke, coming suddenly out of a snooze. 'Someone writin' pretty things to you, what?'

'Charming things,' said Lord Peter.

The Duke eyed him doubtfully.

'Hope to goodness you don't go and marry a chorus beauty,' he muttered inwardly, and returned to *The Times*.

Over dinner I had set myself to discover Cummings's tastes, and found them to run in the direction of the music-hall stage. During his first glass I drew him out in this direction, your lordship having kindly given me opportunities of seeing every performance in London, and I spoke more freely than I should consider becoming in the ordinary way in order to make myself pleasant to him. I may say that his views on women and the stage were such as I should have expected from a man who would smoke with your lordship's port.

With the second glass I introduced the subject of your lordship's inquiries. In order to save time I will write our conversation in the form of a dialogue, as nearly as possible as it actually took place.

Cummings: You seem to get many

opportunities of seeing a bit of life, Mr Bunter.

Bunter: One can always make opportunities if one knows how.

Cummings: Ah, it's very easy for you to talk, Mr Bunter. You're not married, for one thing.

Bunter: I know better than that, Mr Cummings.

Cummings: So do I — *now*, when it's too late. (He sighed heavily, and I filled up his glass.)

Bunter: Does Mrs Cummings live with you at Battersea?

Cummings: Yes, her and me we do for my governor. Such a life! Not but what there's a char comes in by the day. But what's a char? I can tell you it's dull all by ourselves in that d—d Battersea suburb.

Bunter: Not very convenient for the Halls, of course.

Cummings: I believe you. It's all right for you, here in Piccadilly, right on the spot as you might say. And I daresay your governor's often out all night, eh?

Bunter: Oh, frequently, Mr Cummings.

Cummings: And I daresay you take the opportunity to slip off yourself every so often, eh?

Bunter: Well, what do *you* think, Mr Cummings?

Cummings: That's it; there you are! But what's a man to do with a nagging fool of a wife and a blasted scientific doctor for a governor, as sits up all night cutting up dead bodies and experimenting with frogs?

Bunter: Surely he goes out sometimes.

Cummings: Not often. And always back before twelve. And the way he goes on if he rings the bell and you ain't there. I give you *my* word, Mr Bunter.

Bunter: Temper?

Cummings: No-o-o — but looking through you, nasty-like, as if you was on that operating table of his and he was going to cut you up. Nothing a man could rightly complain of, you understand, Mr Bunter, just nasty looks. Not but what I say he's very correct. Apologises if he's been inconsiderate. But what's the good of that when he's been and gone and lost you your night's rest?

Bunter: How does he do that? Keeps you up late, you mean?

Cummings: Not him; far from it. House locked up and household to bed at half-past ten. That's his little rule. Not but what I'm glad enough to go as a rule, it's that dreary. Still, when I *do* go to bed I like to go to sleep.

Bunter: What does he do? Walk about the house?

Cummings: Doesn't he? All night. And in and out of the private door to the hospital.

Bunter: You don't mean to say, Mr Cummings, a great specialist like Sir Julian Freke does night work at the hospital?

Cummings: No, no; he does his own work — research work, as you may say. Cuts

170

people up. They say he's very clever. Could take you or me to pieces like a clock, Mr Bunter, and put us together again.

Bunter: Do you sleep in the basement, then, to hear him so plain?

Cummings: No; our bedroom's at the top. But, Lord! what's that! He'll bang the door so you can hear him all over the house.

Bunter: Ah, many's the time I've had to speak to Lord Peter about that. And talking all night. And baths.

Cummings: Baths? You may well say that, Mr Bunter. Baths? Me and my wife sleep next to the cistern-room. Noise fit to wake the dead. All hours. When d'you think he chose to have a bath? No later than last Monday night, Mr Bunter?

Bunter: I've known them to do it at two in the morning Mr Cummings.

Cummings: Have you, now? Well, this was at three. Three o'clock in the morning we was waked up. I give you *my* word.

Bunter: You don't say so, Mr Cummings.

Cummings: He cuts up diseases, you see, Mr Bunter, and then he don't like to go to bed till he's washed the bacilluses off, if you understand me. Very natural, too, I daresay. But what I say is, the middle of the night's no time for a gentleman to be occupying his mind with diseases.

Bunter: These great men have their own way of doing things.

Cummings: Well, all I can say is, it isn't my way.

171

(I could believe that, your lordship. Cummings has no signs of greatness about him, and his trousers are not what I would wish to see in a man of his profession.)

Bunter: Is he habitually as late as that, Mr Cummings?

Cummings: Well, no, Mr Bunter, I will say, not as a general rule. He apologised, too, in the morning, and said he would have the cistern seen to — and very necessary, in my opinion, for the air gets into the pipes, and the groaning and screeching as goes on is something awful. Just like Niagara, if you follow me, Mr Bunter, I give you *my* word.

Bunter: Well, that's as it should be, Mr Cummings. One can put up with a great deal from a gentleman that has the manners to apologise. And, of course, sometimes they can't help themselves. A visitor will come in unexpectedly and keep them late, perhaps.

Cummings: That's true enough, Mr Bunter. Now I come to think of it, there *was* a gentleman come in on Monday evening. Not that he came late, but he stayed about an hour, and may have put Sir Julian behindhand.

Bunter: Very likely. Let me give you some more port, Mr Cummings. Or a little of Lord Peter's old brandy.

Cummings: A little of the brandy, thank you, Mr Bunter. I suppose you have the run of the cellar here. (He winked at me.)

'Trust me for that,' I said, and I fetched him the Napoleon. I assure your lordship it went to my heart to pour it out for a man like that. However, seeing we had got on the right track, I felt it wouldn't be wasted.

'I'm sure I wish it was always gentlemen that come here at night,' I said. (Your lordship will excuse me, I am sure, making such a suggestion.)

('Good God,' said Lord Peter, 'I wish Bunter was less thorough in his methods.')

Cummings: Oh, he's that sort, his lordship, is he? (He chuckled and poked me. I suppress a portion of his conversation here, which could not fail to be as offensive to your lordship as it was to myself. He went on:) No, it's none of that with Sir Julian. Very few visitors at night, and always gentlemen. And going early as a rule, like the one I mentioned.

Bunter: Just as well. There's nothing I find more wearisome, Mr Cummings, than sitting up to see visitors out.

Cummings: Oh, I didn't see this one out. Sir Julian let him out himself at ten o'clock or thereabouts. I heard the gentleman shout 'Good night' and off he goes.

Bunter: Does Sir Julian always do that?

Cummings: Well, that depends. If he sees visitors downstairs, he lets them out himself; if he sees them upstairs in the library, he rings for me.

Bunter: This was a downstairs visitor, then?

Cummings: Oh, yes. Sir Julian opened the door to him. I remember. He happened to be working in the hall. Though now I come to think of it, they went up to the library afterwards. That's funny, I know they did, because I happened to go up to the hall with coals, and I heard them upstairs. Besides, Sir Julian rang for me in the library a few minutes later. Still, anyway, we heard him go at ten, or it may have been a bit before. He hadn't only stayed about three-quarters of an hour. However, as I was saying, there was Sir Julian banging in and out of the private door all night, and a bath at three in the morning, and up again for breakfast at eight — it beats me. If I had all his money, curse me if I'd go poking about with dead men in the middle of the night. I'd find something better to do with my time, eh, Mr Bunter —

I need not repeat any more of his conversation, as it became unpleasant and incoherent, and I could not bring him back to the events of Monday night. I was unable to get rid of him till three. He cried on my neck and said I was the bird, and you were the governor for him. He said that Sir Julian would be greatly annoyed with him for coming home so late, but Sunday night was his night out and if anything was said about it he would give notice. I think he will be ill-advised to do so, as I feel he is not a man I could conscientiously recommend if I were in Sir Julian Freke's place. I noted that his boot heels were slightly worn down.

I should wish to add, as a tribute to the

174

great merits of your lordship's cellar, that, although I was obliged to drink a somewhat large quantity both of the Cockburn '68 and the 1800 Napoleon, I feel no headache or other ill effects this morning.

Trusting that your lordship is deriving real benefit from the country air, and that the little information I have been able to obtain will prove satisfactory, I remain,

With respectful duty to all the family,

Obediently yours,

MERVYN BUNTER.

'Y'know,' said Lord Peter thoughtfully to himself, 'I sometimes think Mervyn Bunter's pullin' my leg. What is it, Soames?'

'A telegram, my lord.'

'Parker,' said Lord Peter, opening it. It said:

'Description recognised Chelsea Workhouse. Unknown vagrant injured street accident Wednesday week. Died workhouse Monday. Delivered St Luke's same evening by order Freke. Much puzzled. PARKER.'

'Hurray!' said Lord Peter, suddenly sparkling. 'I'm glad I've puzzled Parker. Gives me confidence in myself. Makes me feel like Sherlock Holmes. 'Perfectly simple, Watson.' Dash it all, though! this is a beastly business. Still, it's puzzled Parker.'

'What's the matter?' asked the Duke, getting up and yawning.

'Marching orders,' said Peter, 'back to town. Many thanks for your hospitality, old bird — I'm feelin' no end better. Ready to tackle Professor Moriarty or Leon Kestrel or any of 'em.'

'I do wish you'd keep out of the police courts,' grumbled the Duke. 'It makes it so dashed awkward for me, havin' a brother makin' himself conspicuous.'

'Sorry, Gerald,' said the other, 'I know I'm a beastly blot on the 'scutcheon.'

'Why can't you marry and settle down and live quietly, doin' something useful?' said the Duke, unappeased.

'Because that was a wash-out, as you perfectly well know,' said Peter. 'Besides,' he added cheerfully, 'I'm bein' no end useful. You may come to want me yourself; you never know. When anybody comes blackmailin' you, Gerald, or your first deserted wife turns up unexpectedly from the West Indies, you'll realise the pull of havin' a private detective in the family. 'Delicate private business arranged with tact and discretion. Investigations undertaken. Divorce evidence a speciality. Every guarantee!' Come, now.'

'Ass!' said Lord Denver, throwing the newspaper violently into his armchair. 'When do you want the car?'

'Almost at once. I say, Jerry, I'm taking Mother up with me.'

'Why should she be mixed up in it?'

'Well, I want her help.'

'I call it most unsuitable,' said the Duke.

The Dowager Duchess, however, made no objection.

'I used to know her quite well,' she said, 'when she was Christine Ford. Why, dear?'

176

'Because,' said Lord Peter, 'there's a terrible piece of news to be broken to her about her husband.'

'Is he dead, dear?'

'Yes, and she will have to come and identify him.'

'Poor Christine.'

'Under very revolting circumstances, Mother.'

'I'll come with you, dear.'

'Thank you, Mother, you're a brick. D'you mind gettin' your things on straight away and comin' up with me? I'll tell you about it in the car.'

10

Mr Parker, a faithful though doubting Thomas, had duly secured his medical student: a large young man like an over-grown puppy, with innocent eyes and freckled face. He sat on the Chesterfield before Lord Peter's library fire, bewildered in equal measure by his errand, his surroundings and the drink which he was absorbing. His palate, though untutored, was naturally a good one, and he realised that even to call this liquid a drink — the term ordinarily used by him to designate cheap whisky, postwar beer or a dubious glass of claret in a Soho restaurant — was a sacrilege; this was something outside normal experience: a genie in a bottle.

The man called Parker, whom he had happened to run across the evening before in the public house at the corner of Prince of Wales Road, seemed to be a good sort. He had insisted on bringing him round to see this friend of his, who lived splendidly in Piccadilly. Parker was quite understandable; he put him down as a government servant, or perhaps something in the City. The friend was embarrassing; he was a lord, to begin with, and his clothes were a kind of rebuke to the world at large. He talked the most fatuous nonsense, certainly, but in a disconcerting way. He didn't dig into a joke and get all the fun out of it; he made it in passing, so to speak, and skipped away to something else before your retort was ready. He had a truly terrible man-servant — the sort you read about in books — who froze the marrow in your bones with silent criticism. Parker appeared to bear up under the strain, and this made you think more highly of Parker; he must be more habituated to the surroundings of the great than you would think to look at him. You wondered what the carpet had cost on which Parker was carelessly spilling cigar ash; your father was an upholsterer — Mr Piggott, of Piggott & Piggott, Liverpool — and you knew enough about carpets to know that you couldn't even guess at the price of this one. When you moved your head on the bulging silk cushion in the corner of the sofa, it made you wish you shaved more often and more carefully. The sofa was a monster — but even so, it hardly seemed big enough to contain you. This Lord Peter was not very tall — in fact, he was rather a small man, but he didn't look undersized. He looked right; he made you feel that to be six-foot-three was rather vulgarly assertive; you felt like Mother's new drawing-room curtains — all over great, big blobs. But everybody was very decent to you, and nobody said anything you couldn't understand, or sneered at you. There were some frightfully deep-looking books on the shelves all round, and you had looked into a great folio Dante which was lying on the table, but your hosts were talking quite ordinarily and rationally about the sort of books you read yourself

— clinking good love stories and detective stories. You had read a lot of those, and could give an opinion, and they listened to what you had to say, though Lord Peter had a funny way of talking about books, too, as if the author had confided in him beforehand, and told him how the story was put together, and which bit was written first. It reminded you of the way old Freke took a body to pieces.

'Thing I object to in detective stories,' said Mr Piggott, 'is the way fellows remember every bloomin' thing that's happened to 'em within the last six months. They're always ready with their time of day and was it rainin' or not, and what were they doin' on such an' such a day. Reel it all off like a page of poetry. But one ain't like that in real life, d'you think so, Lord Peter?' Lord Peter smiled and young Piggott instantly embarrassed, appealed to his earlier acquaintance. 'You know what I mean, Parker. Come now. One day's so like another. I'm sure I couldn't remember — well, I might remember yesterday, p'r'aps, but I couldn't be certain about what I was doin' last week if I was to be shot for it.'

'No,' said Parker, 'and evidence given in police statements sounds just as impossible. But they don't really get it like that, you know. I mean, a man doesn't just say, 'Last Friday I went out at 10 a.m. to buy a mutton chop. As I was turning into Mortimer Street I noticed a girl of about twenty-two with black hair and brown eyes, wearing a green jumper, check skirt, Panama hat and black shoes, riding a Royal Sunbeam cycle

180

at about ten miles an hour turning the corner by the Church of St Simon and St Jude on the wrong side of the road riding towards the market place!' It amounts to that, of course, but it's really wormed out of him by a series of questions.'

'And in short stories,' said Lord Peter, 'it has to be put in statement form, because the real conversation would be so long and twaddly and tedious, and nobody would have the patience to read it. Writers have to consider their readers, if any, y'see.'

'Yes,' said Mr Piggott, 'but I bet you most people would find it jolly difficult to remember, even if you ask 'em things. I should — of course, I know I'm a bit of a fool, but then, most people are, ain't they? You know what I mean. Witnesses ain't detectives, they're just average idiots like you and me.'

'Quite so,' said Lord Peter, smiling as the force of the last phrase sank into its unhappy perpetrator: 'you mean, if I were to ask you in a general way what you were doin' — say, a week ago today, you wouldn't be able to tell me a thing about it offhand?'

'No — I'm sure I shouldn't.' He considered. 'No. I was in at the Hospital as usual, I suppose, and, being Tuesday, there'd be a lecture on something or the other — dashed if I know what — and in the evening I went out with Tommy Pringle — no, that must have been Monday — or was it Wednesday? I tell you, I couldn't swear to anything.'

'You do yourself an injustice,' said Lord Peter

gravely. 'I'm sure, for instance, you recollect what work you were doing in the dissecting-room on that day, for example.'

'Lord, no! not for certain. I mean, I daresay it might come back to me if I thought for a long time, but I wouldn't swear to it in a court of law.'

'I'll bet you half-a-crown to sixpence,' said Lord Peter, 'that you'll remember within five minutes.'

'I'm sure I can't.'

'We'll see. Do you keep a notebook of the work you do when you dissect? Drawings or anything?'

'Oh, yes.'

'Think of that. What's the last thing you did in it?'

'That's easy, because I only did it this morning. It was leg muscles.'

'Yes. Who was the subject?'

'An old woman of sorts; died of pneumonia.'

'Yes. Turn back the pages of your drawing book in your mind. What came before that?'

'Oh, some animals — still legs; I'm doing motor muscles at present. Yes. That was old Cunningham's demonstration on comparative anatomy. I did rather a good thing of a hare's leg, and a frog's, and rudimentary legs on a snake.'

'Yes. Which day does Mr Cunningham lecture?'

'Friday.'

'Friday: yes. Turn back again. What comes before that?'

182

Mr Piggott shook his head.

'Do your drawings of legs begin on the right-hand page or the left-hand page? Can you see the first drawing?'

'Yes — yes — I can see the date written at the top. It's a section of a frog's hind leg, on the right-hand page.'

'Yes. Think of the open book in your mind's eye. What is opposite to it?'

This demanded some mental concentration.

'Something round — coloured — oh, yes — it's a hand.'

'Yes. You went on from muscles of the hand and arm to leg-and foot-muscles?'

'Yes; that's right. I've got a set of drawing of arms.'

'Yes. Did you make those on the Thursday?'

'No; I'm never in the dissecting-room on Thursday.'

'On Wednesday, perhaps?'

'Yes; I must have made them on Wednesday. Yes; I did. I went in there after we'd seen those tetanus patients in the morning. I did them on Wednesday afternoon. I know I went back because I wanted to finish 'em. I worked rather hard — for me. That's why I remember.'

'Yes; you went back to finish them. When had you begun them, then?'

'Why, the day before.'

'The day before. That was Tuesday, wasn't it?'

'I've lost count — yes, the day before Wednesday — yes, Tuesday.'

'Yes. Were they a man's arms or a woman's arms?'

'Oh, a man's arms.'

'Yes; last Tuesday, a week ago today, you were dissecting a man's arms in the dissecting-room. Sixpence, please.'

'By Jove!'

'Wait a moment. You know a lot more about it than that. You've no idea how much you know. You know what kind of man he was.'

'Oh, I never saw him complete, you know. I got there a bit late that day, I remember. I'd asked for an arm specially, because I was rather weak in arms, and Watts — that's the attendant — had promised to save me one.'

'Yes. You have arrived late and found your arm waiting for you. You are dissecting it — taking your scissors and slitting up the skin and pinning it back. Was it very young, fair skin?'

'Oh, no — no. Ordinary skin, I think — with dark hairs on it — yes, that was it.'

'Yes. A lean, stringy arm, perhaps, with no extra fat anywhere?'

'Oh, no — I was rather annoyed about that, I wanted a good, muscular arm, but it was rather poorly developed and the fat got in my way.'

'Yes; a sedentary man who didn't do much manual work.'

'That's right.'

'Yes. You dissected the hand, for instance, and made a drawing of it. You would have noticed any hard calluses.'

'Oh, there was nothing of the sort.'

'No. But should you say it was a young man's arm? Firm young flesh and limber joints?'

184

'No — no.'

'No. Old and stringy, perhaps.'

'No. Middle-aged — with rheumatism. I mean, there was a chalky deposit in the joints, and the fingers were a bit swollen.'

'Yes. A man about fifty.'

'About that.'

'Yes. There were other students at work on the same body.'

'Oh, yes.'

'Yes. And they made all the usual sort of jokes about it.'

'I expect so — oh, yes!'

'You can remember some of them. Who is your local funny man, so to speak?'

'Tommy Pringle.'

'What was Tommy Pringle doing?'

'Can't remember.'

'Whereabouts was Tommy Pringle working?'

'Over by the instrument cupboard — by sink C.'

'Yes. Get a picture of Tommy Pringle in your mind's eye.'

Piggott began to laugh.

'I remember now. Tommy Pringle said the old Sheeny — '

'Why did he call him a Sheeny?'

'I don't know. But I know he did.'

'Perhaps he looked like it. Did you see his head?'

'No.'

'Who had the head?'

'I don't know — oh, yes, I do, though. Old Freke bagged the head himself, and little

Bouncible Binns was very cross about it, because he'd been promised a head to do with old Scrooger.'

'I see; what was Sir Julian doing with the head?'

'He called us up and gave us a jaw on spinal haemorrhage and nervous lesions.'

'Yes. Well, go back to Tommy Pringle.'

Tommy Pringle's joke was repeated, not without some embarrassment.

'Quite so. Was that all?'

'No. The chap who was working with Tommy said that sort of thing came from over-feeding.'

'I deduce that Tommy Pringle's partner was interested in the alimentary canal.'

'Yes, and Tommy said, if he'd thought they'd feed you like that he'd go to the workhouse himself.'

'Then the man was a pauper from the workhouse?'

'Well, he must have been, I suppose.'

'Are the workhouse paupers usually fat and well-fed?'

'Well, no — come to think of it, not as a rule.'

'In fact, it struck Tommy Pringle and his friend that this was something a little out of the way in a workhouse subject?'

'Yes.'

'And if the alimentary canal was so entertaining to these gentlemen I imagine the subject had come by his death shortly after a full meal.'

'Yes — oh, yes — he'd have had to, wouldn't he?'

'Well, I don't know,' said Lord Peter. 'That's in

your department, you know. That would be your inference, from what they said.'

'Oh, yes. Undoubtedly.'

'Yes; you wouldn't, for example, expect them to make that observation if the patient had been ill for a long time and fed on slops.'

'Of course not.'

'Well, you see, you really know a lot about it. On Tuesday week you were dissecting the arm muscles of a rheumatic middle-aged Jew, of sedentary habits, who had died shortly after eating a heavy meal, of some injury producing spinal haemorrhage and nervous lesions, and so forth, and who was presumed to come from the workhouse?'

'Yes.'

'And you could swear to those facts, if need were?'

'Well, if you put it that way, I suppose I could.'

'Of course you could.'

Mr Piggott sat for some moments in contemplation.

'I say,' he said at last, 'I did know all that, didn't I?'

'Oh, yes — you knew it all right — like Socrates' slave.'

'Who's he?'

'A person in a book I used to read as a boy.'

'Oh — does he come in *The Last Days of Pompeii*?'

'No — another book — I daresay you escaped it. It's rather dull.'

'I never read much except Henty and Fenlmore Cooper at school . . . But — have I got

187

rather an extra good memory, then?'

'You have a better memory than you credit yourself with.'

'Then why can't I remember all the medical stuff? It all goes out of my head like a sieve.'

'Well, why can't you?' said Lord Peter, standing, on the hearthrug and smiling down at his guest.

'Well,' said the young man, 'the chaps who examine one don't ask the same sort of questions you do.'

'No?'

'No — they leave you to remember all by yourself. And it's beastly hard. Nothing to catch hold of, don't you know? But, I say — how did you know about Tommy Pringle being the funny man and — '

'I didn't, till you told me.'

'No; I know. But how did you know he'd be there if you did ask? I mean to say — I say,' said Mr Piggott, who was becoming mellowed by influences themselves not unconnected with the alimentary canal — 'I say, are you rather clever, or am I rather stupid?'

'No, no,' said Lord Peter, 'it's me, I'm always askin' such stupid questions, everybody thinks I must mean somethin' by 'em.'

This was too involved for Mr Piggott.

'Never mind,' said Parker, soothingly, 'he's always like that. You mustn't take any notice. He can't help it. It's premature senile decay, often observed in the families of hereditary legislators. Go away, Wimsey, and play us the *Beggar's Opera*, or something.'

'That's good enough, isn't it?' said Lord Peter, when the happy Mr Piggott had been despatched home after a really delightful evening.

'I'm afraid so,' said Parker. 'But it seems almost incredible.'

'There's nothing incredible in human nature,' said Lord Peter; 'at least, in educated human nature. Have you got that exhumation order?'

'I shall have it tomorrow. I thought of fixing up with the workhouse people for tomorrow afternoon. I shall have to go and see them first.'

'Right you are. I'll let my mother know.'

'I begin to feel like you, Wimsey, I don't like this job.'

'I like it a deal better than I did.'

'You are really certain we're not making a mistake?'

Lord Peter had strolled across to the window. The curtain was not perfectly drawn, and he stood gazing out through the gap into lighted Piccadilly. At this he turned round:

'If we are,' he said, 'we shall know tomorrow, and no harm will have been done. But I rather think you will receive a certain amount of confirmation on your way home. Look here, Parker, d'you know, if I were you I'd spend the night here. There's a spare bedroom; I can easily put you up.'

Parker stared at him.

'Do you mean — I'm likely to be attacked?'

'I think it very likely indeed.'

'Is there anybody in the street?'

'Not now; there was half an hour ago.'

'When Piggott left?'

'Yes.'

'I say — I hope the boy is in no danger.'

'That's what I went down to see. I don't think so. Fact is, I don't suppose anybody would imagine we'd exactly made a confidant of Piggott. But I think you and I are in danger. You'll stay?'

'I'm damned if I will, Wimsey; why should I run away?'

'Bosh!' said Peter, 'you'd run away all right if you believed me, and why not? You don't believe me. In fact, you're still not certain I'm on the right tack. Go in peace, but don't say I didn't warn you.'

'I won't; I'll dictate a message with my dying breath to say I was convinced.'

'Well, don't walk — take a taxi.'

'Very well, I'll do that.'

'And don't let anybody else get into it.'

'No.'

It was a raw, unpleasant night. A taxi deposited a load of people returning from the theatre at the block of flats next door, and Parker secured it for himself. He was just giving the address to the driver, when a man came hastily running up from a side street. He was in evening dress and an over-coat. He rushed up, signalling frantically.

'Sir — sir! — dear me! why, it's Mr Parker! How fortunate! If you would be so kind — summoned from the club — a sick friend — can't find a taxi — everybody going home from the theatre — if I might share your cab — you are returning to Bloomsbury? I want

Russell Square — if I might presume — a matter of life and death.'

He spoke in hurried gasps, as though he had been running violently and far. Parker promptly stepped out of the taxi.

'Delighted to be of service to you, Sir Julian,' he said; 'take my taxi. I am going down to Craven Street myself, but I'm in no hurry. Pray make use of the cab.'

'It's extremely kind of you,' said the surgeon. 'I am ashamed — '

'That's all right,' said Parker, cheerily. 'I can wait.' He assisted Freke into the taxi. 'What number? 24 Russell Square, driver, and look sharp.'

The taxi drove off. Parker remounted the stairs and rang Lord Peter's bell.

'Thanks, old man,' he said. 'I'll stop the night, after all.'

'Come in,' said Wimsey.

'Did you see that?' asked Parker.

'I saw something. What happened exactly?'

Parker told his story. 'Frankly,' he said, 'I've been thinking you a bit mad, but now I'm not quite so sure of it.'

Peter laughed.

'Blessed are they that have not seen and yet have believed. Bunter, Mr Parker will stay the night.'

'Look here, Wimsey, let's have another look at this business. Where's that letter?'

Lord Peter produced Bunter's essay in dialogue. Parker studied it for a short time in silence.

'You know, Wimsey, I'm as full of objections to this idea as an egg is of meat.'

'So'm I, old son. That's why I want to dig up our Chelsea pauper. But trot out your objections.'

'Well — '

'Well, look here, I don't pretend to be able to fill in all the blanks myself. But here we have two mysterious occurrences in one night, and a complete chain connecting the one with another through one particular person. It's beastly, but it's not unthinkable.'

'Yes, I know all that. But there are one or two quite definite stumbling-blocks.'

'Yes, I know. But, see here. On the one hand, Levy disappeared after being last seen looking for Prince of Wales Road at nine o'clock. At eight next morning a dead man, not unlike him in general outline, is discovered in a bath in Queen Caroline Mansions. Levy, by Freke's own admission, was going to see Freke. By information received from Chelsea workhouse a dead man, answering to the description of the Battersea corpse in its natural state, was delivered that same day to Freke. We have Levy with a past, and no future, as it were; an unknown vagrant with a future (in the cemetery) and no past, and Freke stands between their future and their past.'

'That looks all right — '

'Yes. Now, further: Freke has a motive for getting rid of Levy — an old jealousy.'

'Very old — and not much of a motive.'

'People have been known to do that sort of

192

thing.[1] You're thinking that people don't keep up old jealousies for twenty years or so. Perhaps not. Not just primitive, brute jealousy. That means a word and a blow. But the thing that rankles is hurt vanity. That sticks. Humiliation. And we've all got a sore spot we don't like to have touched. I've got it. You've got it. Some blighter said hell knew no fury like a woman scorned. Stickin' it on to women, poor devils. Sex is every man's loco spot — you needn't fidget, you know it's true — he'll take a disappointment, but not a humiliation. I knew a man once who'd been turned down — not too charitably — by a girl he was engaged to. He spoke quite decently about

---

[1] Lord Peter was not without authority for his opinion: 'With respect to the alleged motive, it is of great importance to see whether there was a motive for committing such a crime, or whether there was not, or whether there is an improbability of its having been committed so strong as not to be over-powered by positive evidence. But *if there be any motive which can be assigned, I am bound to tell you that the inadequacy of that motive is of little importance.* We know, from the experience of criminal courts, that atrocious crimes of this sort have been committed from very slight motives; *not merely from malice and revenge,* but to gain a small pecuniary advantage, and to drive off for a time pressing difficulties.' — L. C. J. Campbell, summing up in Reg. *v.* Palmer, Shorthand Report, p. 308. C.C.C., May 1856, Sess. Pa. 5. (Italics mine. D.L.S.)

her. I asked what had become of her. 'Oh', he said, 'she married the other fellow.' And then burst out — couldn't help himself. 'Lord, yes!' he cried. 'To think of it — jilted for a Scotchman!' I don't know why he didn't like Scots, but that was what got him on the raw. Look at Freke. I've read his books. His attacks on his antagonists are savage. And he's a scientist. Yet he can't bear opposition, even in his work, which is where any first-class man is most sane and open-minded. Do you think he's a man to take a beating from any man on a side-issue? On a man's most sensitive side-issue? People are opinionated about side-issues, you know. I see red if anybody questions my judgement about a book. And Levy — who was nobody twenty years ago — romps in and carries off Freke's girl from under his nose. It isn't the girl Freke would bother about — it's having his aristocratic nose put out of joint by a little Jewish nobody.

'There's another thing. Freke's got another side-issue. He likes crime. In that criminology book of his he gloats over a hardened murderer. I've read it, and I've seen the admiration simply glaring out between the lines whenever he writes about a callous and successful criminal. He reserves his contempt for the victims or the penitents or the men who lose their heads and get found out. His heroes are Edmond de la Pommerais, who persuaded his mistress into becoming an accessory to her own murder, and George Joseph Smith of Brides-in-a-bath fame, who could make passionate love to his wife in the night and carry out his plot to murder her in the morning. After all, he thinks conscience is a sort of vermiform appendix. Chop it out and you'll feel all the better. Freke isn't troubled by the usual conscientious deterrent. Witness his own hand in his books. Now again. The man who went to Levy's house in his place knew the house: Freke knew the house; he was a red-haired man, smaller than Levy, but not much smaller, since he could wear his clothes without appearing ludicrous: you have seen Freke — you know his height — about five-foot-eleven, I suppose, and his auburn mane; he probably wore surgical gloves: Freke is a surgeon; he was a methodical and daring man: surgeons are obliged to be both daring and methodical. Now take the other side. The man who got hold of the Battersea corpse had to have access to dead bodies. Freke obviously had access to dead bodies. He had to be cool and quick and callous about handling a dead body. Surgeons are all that. He had to be a strong man to carry the body across the roofs and dump it in at Thipps's window. Freke is a powerful man and a member of the Alpine Club. He probably wore surgical gloves and he let the body down from the roof with a surgical bandage. This points to a surgeon again. He undoubtedly lived in the neighbourhood. Freke lives next door. The girl you interviewed heard a bump on the roof of the end house. That is the house next to Freke's. Every time we look at Freke, he leads some-where, whereas Milligan and Thipps and Crimplesham and all the other people we've honoured with our suspicion simply led nowhere.'

195

'Yes; but it's not quite so simple as you make out. What was Levy doing in that surreptitious way at Freke's on Monday night?'

'Well, you have Freke's explanation.'

'Rot, Wimsey. You said yourself it wouldn't do.'

'Excellent. It won't do. Therefore Freke was lying. Why should he lie about it, unless he has some object in hiding the truth?'

'Well, but why mention it at all?'

'Because Levy, contrary to all expectation, had been seen at the corner of the road. That was a nasty accident for Freke. He thought it best to be beforehand with an explanation — of sorts. He reckoned, of course, on nobody's ever connecting Levy with Battersea Park.'

'Well, then, we come back to the first question. Why did Levy go there?'

'I don't know, but he was got there somehow. Why did Freke buy all those Peruvian Oil shares?'

'I don't know,' said Parker in his turn.

'Anyway,' went on Wimsey, 'Freke expected him, and made arrangements to let him in himself, so that Cummings shouldn't see who the caller was.'

'But the caller left again at ten.'

'Oh, Charles! I did not expect this of you. This is the purest Suggery! Who saw him go? Somebody said 'Good-night' and walked away down the street. And you believe it was Levy because Freke didn't go out of his way to explain that it wasn't.'

'D'you mean that Freke walked cheerfully out of the house to Park Lane, and left Levy behind

— dead or alive — for Cummings to find?'

'We have Cummings's word that he did nothing of the sort. A few minute after the steps walked away from the house, Freke rang the library bell and told Cummings to shut up for the night.'

'Then — '

'Well — there's a side door to the house, I suppose — in fact, you know there is — Cummings said so — through the hospital.'

'Yes — well, where was Levy?'

'Levy went up into the library and never came down. You've been in Freke's library. Where would you have put him?'

'In my bedroom next door.'

'Then that's where he did put him.'

'But suppose the man went in to turn down the bed?'

'Beds are turned down by the housekeeper, earlier than ten o'clock.'

'Yes . . . But Cummings heard Freke about the house all night.'

'He heard him go in and out two or three times. He'd expect him to do that, anyway.'

'Do you mean to say Freke got all that job finished before three in the morning?'

'Why not?'

'Quick work.'

'Well, call it quick work. Besides, why three? Cummings never saw him again till he called him for eight o'clock breakfast.'

'But he was having a bath at three.'

'I don't say he didn't get back from Park Lane before three. But I don't suppose Cummings went and looked through the bathroom keyhole to see if he was in the bath.'

Parker considered again.

'How about Crimplesham's pince-nez?' he asked.

'That is a bit mysterious,' said Lord Peter.

'And why Thipps's bathroom?'

'Why, indeed? Pure accident, perhaps — or pure devilry.'

'Do you think all this elaborate scheme could have been put together in a night, Wimsey?'

'Far from it. It was conceived as soon as that man who bore a superficial resemblance to Levy came into the workhouse. He had several days.'

'I see.'

'Freke gave himself away at the inquest. He and Grimbold disagreed about the length of the man's illness. If a small man (comparatively speaking) like Grimbold presumes to disagree with a man like Freke, it's because he is sure of his ground.'

'Then — if your theory is sound — Freke made a mistake.'

'Yes. A very slight one. He was guarding, with unnecessary caution, against starting a train of thought in the mind of anybody — say, the workhouse doctor. Up till then he'd been reckoning on the fact that people don't think a second time about anything (a body, say) that's once been accounted for.'

'What made him lose his head?'

'A chain of unforeseen accidents. Levy's having been recognised — my mother's son having foolishly advertised in *The Times* his connection with the Battersea end of the mystery — Inspector Parker (whose photograph has been a little prominent in the illustrated press lately) seen sitting next door to the Duchess of Denver at the inquest. His aim in life was to prevent the two ends of the problem from linking up. And there were two of the links, literally side by side. Many criminals are wrecked by over-caution.'

Parker was silent.

11

'A regular pea-souper, by Jove,' said Lord Peter.

Parker grunted, and struggled irritably into an overcoat.

'If affords me, if I may say so, the greatest satisfaction,' continued the noble lord, 'that in a collaboration like ours all the uninteresting and disagreeable routine work is done by you.'

Parker grunted again.

'Do you anticipate any difficulty about the warrant?' inquired Lord Peter.

Parker grunted a third time.

'I suppose you've seen to it that all this business is kept quiet?'

'Of course.'

'You've muzzled the workhouse people?'

'Of course.'

'And the police?'

'Yes.'

'Because, if you haven't there'll probably be nobody to arrest.'

'My dear Wimsey, do you think I'm a fool?'

'I had no such hope.'

Parker grunted finally and departed.

Lord Peter settled down to a perusal of his Dante. It afforded him no solace. Lord Peter was hampered in his career as a private detective by a public-school education. Despite Parker's admonitions, he was not always able to discount it. His mind had been warped in its young growth by

'Raffles' and 'Sherlock Holmes', or the senti-
ments for which they stand. He belonged to a
family which had never shot a fox.

'I am an amateur,' said Lord Peter.

Nevertheless, while communing with Dante,
he made up his mind.

★ ★ ★

In the afternoon he found himself in Harley
Street. Sir Julian Freke might be consulted about
one's nerves from two till four on Tuesdays and
Fridays. Lord Peter rang the bell.

'Have you an appointment, sir?' inquired the
man who opened the door.

'No,' said Lord Peter, 'but will you give Sir
Julian my card? I think it possible he may see me
without one.'

He sat down in the beautiful room in which
Sir Julian's patients awaited his healing counsel.
It was full of people. Two or three fashionably
dressed women were discussing shops and
servants together, and teasing a toy griffon. A
big, worried-looking man by himself in a corner
looked at his watch twenty times a minute. Lord
Peter knew him by sight. It was Wintrington, a
millionaire, who had tried to kill himself a few
months ago. He controlled the finances of five
countries, but he could not control his nerves.
The finances of five countries were in Sir Julian
Freke's capable hands. By the fireplace sat a
soldierly-looking young man, of about Lord
Peter's own age. His face was prematurely lined
and worn; he sat bolt upright, his restless eyes

darting in the direction of every slightest sound. On the sofa was an elderly woman of modest appearance, with a young girl. The girl seemed listless and wretched; the woman's look showed deep affection, and anxiety tempered with a timid hope. Close beside Lord Peter was another younger woman, with a little girl, and Lord Peter noticed in both of them the broad cheekbones and beautiful grey, slanting eyes of the Slav. The child, moving restlessly about, trod on Lord Peter's patent-leather toe, and the mother admonished her in French before turning to apologise to Lord Peter.

'Mais je vous en prie, madame,' said the young man, 'it is nothing.'

'She is nervous, pauvre petite,' said the young woman.

'You are seeking advice for her?'

'Yes. He is wonderful, the doctor. Figure to yourself, monsieur, she cannot forget, poor child, the things she has seen.' She leaned nearer, so that the child might not hear. 'We have escaped — from starving Russia — six months ago. I dare not tell you — she has such quick ears, and then, the cries, the tremblings, the convulsions — they all begin again. We were skeletons when we arrived — mon Dieu! — but that is better now. See, she is thin, but she is not starved. She would be fatter but for the nerves that keep her from eating. We who are older, we forget — enfin, on apprend à ne pas y penser — but these children! When one is young, monsieur, tout ça impressionne trop.'

Lord Peter, escaping from the thraldom of

British good form, expressed himself in that language in which sympathy is not condemned to mutism.

'But she is much better, much better,' said the mother proudly, 'the great doctor, he does marvels.'

'C'est un homme précieux,' said Lord Peter.

'Ah, monsieur, c'est un saint qui opère des miracles! Nous prions pour lui, Natasha et moi, tous les jours. N'est-ce pas, chérie? And consider, monsieur, that he does it all, ce grand homme, cet homme illustre, for nothing at all. When we come here, we have not even the clothes upon our backs — we are ruined, famished. Et avec ça que nous sommes de bonne famille — mais hélas! monsieur, en Russie, comme vous savez, ça ne vous vaut que des insultes — des atrocités. Enfin! the great Sir Julian sees us, he says — 'Madame, your little girl is very interesting to me. Say no more. I cure her for nothing — pour ses beaux yeux,' a-t-il ajouté en riant. Ah, monsieur, c'est un saint, un véritable saint! and Natasha is much, much better.'

'Madame, je vous en félicite.'

'And you, monsieur? You are young, well, strong — you also suffer? Is it still the war, perhaps?'

'A little remains of shell-shock,' said Lord Peter.

'Ah, yes. So many good, brave, young men — '

'Sir Julian can spare you a few minutes, my lord, if you will come in now,' said the servant.

Lord Peter bowed to his neighbour, and

walked across the waiting-room. As the door of the consulting-room closed behind him, he remembered having once gone, disguised, into the staff-room of a German officer. He experienced the same feeling — the feeling of being caught in a trap, and a mingling of bravado and shame.

★ ★ ★

He had seen Sir Julian Freke several times from a distance, but never close. Now, while carefully and quite truthfully detailing the circumstances of his recent nervous attack, he considered the man before him. A man taller than himself, with immense breadth of shoulder, and wonderful hands. A face beautiful, impassioned and inhuman; fanatical, compelling eyes, bright blue amid the ruddy bush of hair and beard. They were not the cool and kindly eyes of the family doctor, they were the brooding eyes of the inspired scientist, and they searched one through.

'Well,' thought Lord Peter, 'I shan't have to be explicit, anyhow.'

'Yes,' said Sir Julian, 'yes. You had been working too hard. Puzzling your mind. Yes. More than that, perhaps — troubling your mind, shall we say?'

'I found myself faced with a very alarming contingency.'

'Yes. Unexpectedly, perhaps.'

'Very unexpectedly indeed.'

'Yes. Following on a period of mental and physical strain.'

'Well — perhaps. Nothing out of the way.'

'Yes. The unexpected contingency was — personal to yourself?'

'It demanded an immediate decision as to my own actions — yes, in that sense it was certainly personal.'

'Quite so. You would have to assume some responsibility, no doubt.'

'A very grave responsibility.'

'Affecting others beside yourself?'

'Affecting one other person vitally, and a very great number indirectly.'

'Yes. The time was night. You were sitting in the dark?'

'Not at first. I think I put the light out afterwards.'

'Quite so — that action would naturally suggest itself to you. Were you warm?'

'I think the fire had died down. My man tells me that my teeth were chattering when I went in to him.'

'Yes. You live in Piccadilly?'

'Yes.'

'Heavy traffic sometimes goes past during the night, I expect.'

'Oh, frequently.'

'Just so. Now this decision you refer to — you had taken that decision.'

'Yes.'

'Your mind was made up?'

'Oh, yes.'

'You had decided to take the action, whatever it was.'

'Yes.'

'Yes. It involved perhaps a period of inaction.'

'Of comparative inaction — yes.'

'Of suspense, shall we say?'

'Yes — of suspense, certainly.'

'Possibly of some danger?'

'I don't know that that was in my mind at the time.'

'No — it was a case in which you could not possibly consider yourself.'

'If you like to put it that way.'

'Quite so. Yes. You had these attacks frequently in 1918?'

'Yes — I was very ill for some months.'

'Quite. Since then they have recurred less frequently?'

'Much less frequently.'

'Yes — when did the last occur?'

'About nine months ago.'

'Under what circumstances?'

'I was being worried by certain family matters. It was a question of deciding about some investments, and I was largely responsible.'

'Yes. You were interested last year, I think, in some police case?'

'Yes — in the recovery of Lord Attenbury's emerald necklace.'

'That involved some severe mental exercise?'

'I suppose so. But I enjoyed it very much.'

'Yes. Was the exertion of solving the problem attended by any bad results physically?'

'None.'

'No. You were interested, but not distressed.'

'Exactly.'

'Yes. You have been engaged in other

investigations of the kind?'

'Yes. Little ones.'

'With bad results for your health?'

'Not a bit of it. On the contrary. I took up these cases as a sort of distraction. I had a bad knock just after the war, which didn't make matters any better for me, don't you know.'

'Ah! you are not married?'

'No.'

'No. Will you allow me to make an examination? Just come a little nearer to the light. I want to see your eyes. Whose advice have you had till now?'

'Sir James Hodges'.'

'Ah! yes — he was a sad loss to the medical profession. A really great man — a true scientist. Yes. Thank you. Now I should like to try you with this little invention.'

'What's it do?'

'Well — it tells me about your nervous reactions. Will you sit here?'

The examination that followed was purely medical. When it was concluded, Sir Julian said:

'Now, Lord Peter, I'll tell you about yourself in quite untechnical language — '

'Thanks,' said Peter, 'that's kind of you. I'm an awful fool about long words.'

'Yes. Are you fond of private theatricals, Lord Peter?'

'Not particularly,' said Peter, genuinely surprised. 'Awful bore as a rule. Why?'

'I thought you might be,' said the specialist, drily. 'Well, now. You know quite well that the strain you put on your nerves during the war has left its mark on you. It has left what I may call old wounds in your brain. Sensations received by your nerve-endings sent messages to your brain, and produced minute physical changes there — changes we are only beginning to be able to detect, even with our most delicate instruments. These changes in their turn set up sensations; or I should say, more accurately, that sensations are the names we give to those changes of tissue when we perceive them: we call them horror, fear, sense of responsibility and so on.'

'Yes, I follow you.'

'Very well. Now, if you stimulate those damaged places in your brain again, you run the risk of opening up the old wounds. I mean, that if you get nerve-sensations of any kind producing the reactions which we call horror, fear, and sense of responsibility, they may go on to make disturbance right along the old channel, and produce in their turn physical changes which you will call by the names you were accustomed to associate with them — dread of German mines, responsibility for the lives of your men, strained attention and the inability to distinguish small sounds through the overpowering noise of guns.'

'I see.'

'This effect would be increased by extraneous circumstances producing other familiar physical sensations — night, cold or the rattling of heavy traffic, for instance.'

'Yes.'

'Yes. The old wounds are nearly healed, but not quite. The ordinary exercise of your mental faculties has no bad effect. It is only when you excite the injured part of your brain.'

'Yes, I see.'

'Yes. You must avoid these occasions. You must learn to be irresponsible, Lord Peter.'

'My friends say I'm only too irresponsible already.'

'Very likely. A sensitive nervous temperament often appears so, owing to its mental nimbleness.'

'Oh!'

'Yes. This particular responsibility you were speaking of still rests upon you?'

'Yes, it does.'

'You have not yet completed the course of action on which you have decided?'

'Not yet.'

'You feel bound to carry it through?'

'Oh, yes — I can't back out of it now.'

'No. You are expecting further strain?'

'A certain amount.'

'Do you expect it to last much longer?'

'Very little longer now.'

'Ah! Your nerves are not all they should be.'

'No?'

'No. Nothing to be alarmed about, but you must exercise care while undergoing this strain, and afterwards you should take a complete rest. How about a voyage in the Mediterranean or the South Seas or somewhere?'

'Thanks. I'll think about it.'

'Meanwhile, to carry you over the immediate trouble I will give you something to strengthen your nerves. It will do you no permanent good, you understand, but it will tide you over the bad time. And I will give you a prescription.'

'Thank you.'

Sir Julian got up and went into a small surgery leading out of the consulting-room. Lord Peter watched him moving about — boiling something and writing. Presently he returned with a paper and a hypodermic syringe.

'Here is the prescription. And now, if you will just roll up your sleeve, I will deal with the necessity of the immediate moment.'

Lord Peter obediently rolled up his sleeve. Sir Julian Freke selected a portion of his forearm and anointed it with iodine.

'What's that you're goin' to stick into me? Bugs?'

The surgeon laughed.

'Not exactly,' he said. He pinched up a portion of flesh between his finger and thumb. 'You've had this kind of thing before, I expect.'

'Oh, yes,' said Lord Peter. He watched the cool fingers, fascinated, and the steady approach of the needle. 'Yes — I've had it before — and, d'you know — I don't care frightfully about it.'

He had brought up his right hand, and it closed over the surgeon's wrist like a vice.

The silence was like a shock. The blue eyes did not waver; they burned down steadily upon the heavy white lids below them. Then these slowly lifted; the grey eyes met the blue — coldly, steadily — and held them.

When lovers embrace, there seems no sound in the world but their own breathing. So the two men breathed face to face.

'As you like, of course, Lord Peter,' said Sir Julian, courteously.

'Afraid I'm rather a silly ass,' said Lord Peter, 'but I never could abide these little gadgets. I had one once that went wrong and gave me a rotten bad time. They make me a bit nervous.'

'In that case,' replied Sir Julian, 'it would certainly be better not to have the injection. It might rouse up just those sensations which we are desirous of avoiding. You will take the prescription, then, and do what you can to lessen the immediate strain as far as possible.'

'Oh, yes — I'll take it easy, thanks,' said Lord Peter. He rolled his sleeve down neatly. 'I'm much obliged to you. If I have any further trouble I'll look in again.'

'Do — do — ' said Sir Julian, cheerfully. 'Only make an appointment another time. I'm rather rushed these days. I hope your mother is quite well. I saw her the other day at that Battersea inquest. You should have been there. It would have interested you.'

12

The vile, raw fog tore your throat and ravaged your eyes. You could not see your feet. You stumbled in your walk over poor men's graves.

The feel of Parker's old trench-coat beneath your fingers was comforting. You had felt it in worse places. You clung on now for fear you should get separated. The dim people moving in front of you were like Brocken spectres.

'Take care, gentlemen,' said a toneless voice out of the yellow darkness, 'there's an open grave just hereabouts.'

You bore away to the right, and floundered in a mass of freshly turned clay.

'Hold up, old man,' said Parker.

'Where is Lady Levy?'

'In the mortuary; the Duchess of Denver is with her. Your mother is wonderful, Peter.'

'Isn't she?' said Lord Peter.

A dim blue light carried by somebody ahead wavered and stood still.

'Here you are,' said a voice.

Two Dantesque shapes with pitchforks loomed up.

'Have you finished?' asked somebody.

'Nearly done, sir.' The demons fell to work again with the pitchforks — no, spades.

Somebody sneezed. Parker located the sneezer and introduced him.

'Mr Levett represents the Home Secretary.

Lord Peter Wimsey. We are sorry to drag you out on such a day, Mr Levett.'

'It's all in the day's work,' said Mr Levett, hoarsely. He was muffled to the eyes.

The sound of the spades for many minutes. An iron noise of tools thrown down. Demons stooping and straining.

A black-bearded spectre at your elbow. Introduced. The Master of the Workhouse.

'A very painful matter, Lord Peter. You will forgive me for hoping you and Mr Parker may be mistaken.'

'I should like to be able to hope so, too.'

Something heaving, straining, coming up out of the ground.

'Steady, men. This way. Can you see? Be careful of the graves — they lie pretty thick hereabouts. Are you ready?'

'Right you are, sir. You go with the lantern. We can follow you.'

Lumbering footsteps. Catch hold of Parker's trench-coat again. 'That you, old man? Oh, I beg your pardon, Mr Levett — thought you were Parker.'

'Hullo, Wimsey — here you are.'

More graves. A headstone shouldered crookedly aslant. A trip and jerk over the edge of the rough grass. The squeal of gravel under your feet.

'This way, gentlemen, mind the step.'

The mortuary. Raw red brick and sizzling gas-jets. Two women in black, and Dr Grimbold. The coffin laid on the table with a heavy thump.

''Ave you got that there screwdriver, Bill?

213

Thank 'ee. Be keerful wi' the chisel now. Not much substance to these 'ere boards, sir.'

Several long creaks. A sob. The Duchess's voice, kind but peremptory.

'Hush, Christine. You mustn't cry.'

A mutter of voices. The lurching departure of the Dante demons — good, decent demons in corduroy.

Dr Grimbold's voice — cool and detached as if in the consulting-room.

'Now — have you got that lamp, Mr Wingate? Thank you. Yes, here on the table, please. Be careful not to catch your elbow in the flex, Mr Levett. It would be better, I think, if you came on this side. Yes — yes — thank you. That's excellent.'

The sudden brilliant circle of an electric lamp over the table. Dr Grimbold's beard and spectacles. Mr Levett blowing his nose. Parker bending close. The Master of the Workhouse peering over him. The rest of the room in the enhanced dimness of the gas-jets and the fog.

A low murmur of voices. All heads bent over the work.

Dr Grimbold again — beyond the circle of the lamplight.

'We don't want to distress you unnecessarily, Lady Levy. If you will just tell us what to look for — the — ? Yes, yes, certainly — and — yes — stopped with gold? Yes — the lower jaw, the last but one on the right? Yes — no teeth missing — no — yes? What kind of mole? Yes — just over the left breast? Oh, I beg your pardon, just under — yes — appendicitis? Yes — a long one — yes

214

— in the middle? Yes, I quite understand — a scar on the arm? Yes, I don't know if we shall be able to find that — yes — any little constitutional weakness that might — ? Oh, yes — arthritis — yes — thank you, Lady Levy, that's very clear. Don't come unless I ask you to. Now, Wingate.'

A pause. A murmur. 'Pulled out? After death, you think — well, so do I. Where is Dr Colegrove? You attended this man in the workhouse? Yes. Do you recollect — ? No? You're quite certain about that? Yes — we mustn't make a mistake, you know. Yes, but there are reasons why Sir Julian can't be present; I'm asking *you*, Dr Colegrove. Well, you're certain — that's all I want to know. Just bring the light closer, Mr Wingate, if you please. These miserable shells let the damp in so quickly. Ah! what do you make of this? Yes — yes — well, that's rather unmistakable, isn't it? Who did the head? Oh, Freke — of course. I was going to say they did good work at St Luke's. Beautiful, isn't it, Dr Colegrove? A wonderful surgeon — I saw him when he was at Guy's. Oh, no, gave it up years ago. Nothing like keeping your hand in. Ah — yes, undoubtedly that's it. Have you a towel handy, sir? Thank you. Over the head, if you please — I think we might have another here. Now, Lady Levy — I am going to ask you to look at a scar, and see if you recognise it. I'm sure you are going to help us by being very firm. Take your time — you won't see anything more than you absolutely must.'

'Lucy, don't leave me.'

'No, dear.'

A space cleared at the table. The lamplight on

the Duchess's white hair.

'Oh, yes — oh, yes! No, no — I couldn't be mistaken. There's that funny little kink in it. I've seen it hundreds of times. Oh, Lucy — Reuben!'

'Only a moment more, Lady Levy. The mole — '

'I — I think so — oh, yes, that is the very place.'

'Yes. And the scar — was it three-cornered, just above the elbow?'

'Yes, oh, yes.'

'Is this it?'

'Yes — yes — '

'I must ask you definitely, Lady Levy. Do you, from these three marks identify the body as that of your husband?'

'Oh! I must, mustn't I? Nobody else could have them just the same in just those places? It is my husband. It is Reuben. Oh — '

'Thank you, Lady Levy. You have been very brave and very helpful.'

'But — I don't understand yet. How did he come here? Who did this dreadful thing?'

'Hush, dear,' said the Duchess, 'the man is going to be punished.'

'Oh, but — how cruel! Poor Reuben! Who could have wanted to hurt him? Can I see his face?'

'No, dear,' said the Duchess. 'That isn't possible. Come away — you mustn't distress the doctors and people.'

'No — no — they've all been so kind. Oh, Lucy!'

'We'll go home, dear. You don't want us any

more, Dr Grimbold?'

'No, Duchess, thank you. We are very grateful to you and to Lady Levy for coming.'

There was a pause, while the two women went out. Parker, collected and helpful, escorted them to their waiting car. Then Dr Grimbold again:

'I think Lord Peter Wimsey ought to see — the correctness of his deductions — Lord Peter — very painful — you may wish to see — yes, I was uneasy at the inquest — yes — Lady Levy — remarkably clear evidence — yes — most shocking case — ah, here's Mr Parker — you and Lord Peter Wimsey entirely justified — do I really understand — ? Really? I can hardly believe it — so distinguished a man — as you say, when a great brain turns to crime — yes — look here! Marvellous work — marvellous — somewhat obscured by this time, of course — but the most beautiful sections — here, you see, the left hemisphere — and here — through the corpus striatum — here again — the very track of the damage done by the blow — wonderful — guessed it — saw the effect of the blow as he struck it, you know — ah, I should like to see *his* brain, Mr Parker — and to think that — heavens, Lord Peter, you don't know what a blow you have struck at the whole profession — the whole civilised world! Oh, my dear sir! Can you ask me? My lips are sealed of course — all our lips are sealed.'

The way back through the burial ground. Fog again, and the squeal of wet gravel.

'Are your men ready, Charles?'

'They have gone. I sent them off when I saw

Lady Levy to the car.'

'Who is with them?'

'Sugg.'

'Sugg?'

'Yes — poor devil. They've had him up on the mat at headquarters for bungling the case. All that evidence of Thipps's about the night club was corroborated, you know. That girl he gave the gin-and-bitters to was caught, and came and identified him, and they decided their case wasn't good enough, and let Thipps and the Horrocks girl go. Then they told Sugg he had overstepped his duty and ought to have been more careful. So he ought, but he can't help being a fool. I was sorry for him. It may do him some good to be in at the death. After all, Peter, you and I had special advantages.'

'Yes. Well, it doesn't matter. Whoever goes won't get there in time. Sugg's as good as another.'

But Sugg — an experience rare in his career — was in time.

★   ★   ★

Parker and Lord Peter were at 110A Piccadilly. Lord Peter was playing Bach and Parker was reading Origen when Sugg was announced.

'We've got our man, sir,' said he.

'Good God!' said Peter. 'Alive?'

'We were just in time, my lord. We rang the bell and marched straight up past his man to the library. He was sitting there doing some writing. When we came in, he made a grab for his

218

hypodermic, but we were too quick for him, my lord. We didn't mean to let him slip through our hands, having got so far. We searched him thoroughly and marched him off.'

'He is actually in gaol, then?'

'Oh, yes — safe enough — with two warders to see he doesn't make away with himself.'

'You surprise me, Inspector. Have a drink.'

'Thank you, my lord. I may say that I'm very grateful to you — this case was turning out a pretty bad egg for me. If I was rude to your lordship — '

'Oh, it's all right, Inspector,' said Lord Peter, hastily. 'I don't see how you could possibly have worked it out. I had the good luck to know something about it from other sources.'

'That's what Freke says.' Already the great surgeon was a common criminal in the inspector's eyes — a mere surname. 'He was writing a full confession when we got hold of him, addressed to your lordship. The police will have to have it, of course, but seeing it's written for you, I brought it along for you to see first. Here it is.'

He handed Lord Peter a bulky document.

'Thanks,' said Peter. 'Like to hear it, Charles?'

'Rather.'

Accordingly Lord Peter read it aloud.

13

Dear Lord Peter, — When I was a young man I used to play chess with an old friend of my father's. He was a very bad, and a very slow, player, and he could never see when a checkmate was inevitable, but insisted on playing every move out. I never had any patience with that kind of attitude, and I will freely admit now that the game is yours. I must either stay at home and be hanged or escape abroad and live in an idle and insecure obscurity. I prefer to acknowledge defeat.

If you have read my book on *Criminal Lunacy*, you will remember that I wrote: 'In the majority of cases, the criminal betrays himself by some abnormality attendant upon this pathological condition of the nervous tissues. His mental instability shows itself in various forms: an over-weening vanity, leading him to brag of his achievement; a disproportionate sense of the importance of the offence, resulting from the hallucination of religion, and driving him to confession; egomania, producing the sense of horror or conviction of sin, and driving him to headlong flight without covering his tracks; a reckless confidence, resulting in the neglect of the most ordinary precautions, as in the case of Henry

Wainwright, who left a boy in charge of the murdered woman's remains while he went to call a cab, or on the other hand, a nervous distrust of apperceptions in the past, causing him to revisit the scene of the crime to assure himself that all traces have been as safely removed as *his own judgement knows them to be.* I will not besitate to assert that a perfectly sane man, not intimidated by religious or other delusions, could always render himself perfectly secure from detection, provided, that is, that the crime were sufficiently premeditated and that he were not pressed for time or thrown out in his calculations by purely fortuitous coincidence.

You know as well as I do how far I have made this assertion good in practice. The two accidents which betrayed me I could not by any possibility have foreseen. The first was the chance recognition of Levy by the girl in the Battersea Park Road, which suggested a connection between the two problems. The second was that Thipps should have arranged to go down to Denver on the Tuesday morning, thus enabling your mother to get word of the matter through to you before the body was removed by the police and to suggest a motive for the murder out of what she knew of my previous personal history. If I had been able to destroy these two accidentally forged links of circumstance, I will venture to say that you would never have so much as suspected me, still less obtained sufficient evidence to convict.

Of all human emotions, except perhaps those of hunger and fear, the sexual appetite produces the most violent, and, under some circumstances, the most persistent reactions; I think, however, I am right in saying that at the time when I wrote my book, my original sensual impulse to kill Sir Reuben Levy had already become profoundly modified by my habits of thought. To the animal lust to slay and the primitive human desire for revenge, there was added the rational intention of substantiating my own theories for the satisfaction of myself and the world. If all had turned out as I had planned, I should have deposited a sealed account of my experiment with the Bank of England, instructing my executors to publish it after my death. Now that accident has spoiled the completeness of my demonstration, I entrust the account to you, whom it cannot fail to interest, with the request that you will make it known among scientific men, in justice to my professional reputation.

The really essential factors of success in any undertaking are money and opportunity, and as a rule, the man who can make the first can make the second. During my early career, though I was fairly well-off, I had not absolute command of circumstance. Accordingly I devoted myself to my profession, and contented myself with keeping up a friendly connection with Reuben Levy and his family. This enabled me to remain in touch with his fortunes and interests, so that, when the moment for action should arrive, I might know what weapons to use.

Meanwhile, I carefully studied criminology in fiction and fact — my work on *Criminal Lunacy* was a side-product of this activity — and saw how, in every murder, the real crux of the problem was the disposal of the body. As a doctor, the means of death were always ready to my hand, and I was not likely to make any error in that connection. Nor was I likely to betray myself on account of any illusory sense of wrong-doing. The sole difficulty would be that of destroying all connection between my personality and that of the corpse. You will remember that Michael Finsbury, in Stevenson's entertaining romance, observes. 'What hangs people is the unfortunate circumstance of guilt.' It became clear to me that the mere leaving about of a superfluous corpse could convict nobody, provided that nobody was guilty in connection *with that particular corpse.* Thus the idea of substituting the one body for the other was early arrived at, though it was not till I obtained the practical direction of St Luke's Hospital that I found myself perfectly unfettered in the choice and handling of dead bodies. From this period on, I kept a careful watch on all the material brought in for dissection.

My opportunity did not present itself until the week before Sir Reuben's disappearance, when the medical officer at the Chelsea workhouse sent word to me that an unknown vagrant had been injured that morning by the fall of a piece of scaffolding, and was exhibiting some very interesting nervous and cerebral reactions. I went round and saw the case, and was immediately struck by the man's strong superficial resemblance to Sir Reuben. He had been heavily struck on the back of the neck, dislocating the fourth and fifth cervical vertebrae and heavily bruising the spinal cord. It seemed highly unlikely that he could ever recover, either mentally or physically, and in any case there appeared to me to be no object in indefinitely prolonging so unprofitable an existence. He had obviously been able to support life until recently, as he was fairly well nourished, but the state of his feet and clothing showed that he was unemployed, and under present conditions he was likely to remain so. I decided that he would suit my purpose very well, and immediately put in train certain transactions in the City which I had already sketched out in my own mind. In the meantime, the reactions mentioned by the workhouse doctor were interesting, and I made careful studies of them, and arranged for the delivery of the body to the hospital when I should have completed my preparations.

On the Thursday and Friday of that week

I made private arrangements with various brokers to buy the stock of certain Peruvian oilfields, which had gone down almost to waste-paper. This part of my experiment did not cost me very much, but I contrived to arouse considerable curiosity, and even a mild excitement. At this point I was of course careful not to let my name appear. The incidence of Saturday and Sunday gave me some anxiety lest my man should after all die before I was ready for him, but by the use of saline injections I contrived to keep him alive and, late on Sunday night, he even manifested disquieting symptoms of at any rate a partial recovery.

On Monday morning the market in Peruvians opened briskly. Rumours had evidently got about that somebody knew something, and this day I was not the only buyer in the market. I bought a couple of hundred more shares in my own name, and left the matter to take care of itself. At lunch time I made my arrangements to run into Levy accidentally at the corner of the Mansion House. He expressed (as I expected) his surprise at seeing me in that part of London. I simulated some embarrassment and suggested that we should lunch together. I dragged him to a place a bit off the usual beat, and there ordered a good wine and drank of it as much as he might suppose sufficient to induce a confidential mood. I asked him how things were going on 'Change. He said, 'Oh, all

225

right,' but appeared a little doubtful, and asked me whether I did anything in that way. I said I had a little flutter occasionally, and that, as a matter of fact, I'd been put on to rather a good thing. I glanced round apprehensively at this point, and shifted my chair nearer to his.

'I suppose you don't know anything about Peruvian oil do you?' he said.

I started and looked around again, and leaning across to him, said, dropping my voice.

'Well, I do, as a matter of fact, but I don't want it to get about. I stand to make a good bit on it.'

'But I thought the thing was hollow,' he said; 'it hasn't paid a dividend for umpteen years.'

'No,' I said, 'it hasn't, but it's going to. I've got inside information.' He looked a bit unconvinced, and I emptied off my glass, and edged right up to his ear.

'Look here,' I said, 'I'm not giving this away to everyone, but I don't mind doing you and Christine a good turn. You know, I've always kept a soft place in my heart for her, ever since the old days. You got in ahead of me that time, and now it's up to me to heap coals of fire on you both.'

I was a little excited by this time, and he thought I was drunk.

'It's very kind of you, old man,' he said, 'but I'm a cautious bird, you know, always was. I'd like a bit of proof.'

And he shrugged up his shoulders and looked like a pawnbroker.

'I'll give it to you,' I said, 'but it isn't safe here. Come round to my place tonight after dinner, and I'll show you the report.'

'How d'you get hold of it?' said he.

'I'll tell you tonight,' said I. 'Come round after dinner — any time after nine, say.'

'To Harley Street?' he asked, and I saw that he meant coming.

'No,' I said, 'to Battersea — Prince of Wales Road; I've got some work to do at the hospital. And look here,' I said, 'don't you let on to a soul that you're coming. I bought a couple of hundred shares today, in my own name, and people are sure to get wind of it. If we're known to be about together, someone'll twig something. In fact, it's anything but safe talking about it in this place.'

'All right,' he said, 'I won't say a word to anybody. I'll turn up about nine o'clock. You're sure it's a sound thing?'

'It can't go wrong,' I assured him. And I meant it.

We parted after that, and I went round to the workhouse. My man had died at about eleven o'clock. I had seen him just after breakfast, and was not surprised. I completed the usual formalities with the workhouse authorities, and arranged for his delivery at the hospital about seven o'clock.

In the afternoon, as it was not one of my days to be in Harley Street, I looked up an

227

old friend who lives close to Hyde Park, and found that he was just off to Brighton on some business or other. I had tea with him, and saw him off by the 5.35 from Victoria. On issuing from the barrier it occurred to me to purchase an evening paper, and I thoughtlessly turned my steps to the bookstall. The usual crowds were rushing to catch suburban trains home, and on moving away I found myself involved in a contrary stream of travellers coming up out of the Underground, or bolting from all sides for the 5.45 to Battersea Park and Wandsworth Common. I disengaged myself after some buffeting and went home in a taxi and it was not till I was safely seated there that I discovered somebody's gold-rimmed pince-nez involved in the astrakhan collar of my overcoat. The time from 6.15 to seven I spent concocting something to look like a bogus report for Sir Reuben.

At seven I went through to the hospital, and found the workhouse van just delivering my subject at the side door. I had him taken straight up to the theatre, and told the attendant, William Watts, that I intended to work there that night. I told him I would prepare the body myself — the injection of a preservative would have been a most regrettable complication. I sent him about his business, and then went home and had dinner. I told my man that I should be working in the hospital that evening, and that he could go to bed at 10.30 as usual, as

I could not tell whether I should be late or not. He is used to my erratic ways. I only keep two servants in the Battersea house — the manservant and his wife, who cooks for me. The rougher domestic work is done by a charwoman, who sleeps out. The servants' bedroom is at the top of the house, overlooking Prince of Wales Road.

As soon as I had dined I established myself in the hall with some papers. My man had cleared dinner by a quarter past eight, and I told him to give me the syphon and tantalus; and sent him downstairs. Levy rang the bell at twenty minutes past nine, and I opened the door to him myself. My man appeared at the other end of the hall, but I called to him that it was all right, and he went away. Levy wore an overcoat with evening dress and carried an umbrella. 'Why, how wet you are!' I said. 'How did you come?' 'By bus,' he said, 'and the fool of a conductor forgot to put me down at the end of the road. It's pouring cats and dogs and pitch-dark — I couldn't see where I was.' I was glad he hadn't taken a taxi, but I had rather reckoned on his not doing so. 'Your little economies will be the death of you one of these days,' I said. I was right there, but I hadn't reckoned on their being the death of me as well. I say again, I could not have foreseen it.

I sat him down by the fire, and gave him a whisky. He was in high spirits about some deal in Argentines he was bringing off the

229

next day. We talked money for about a quarter of an hour and then he said:

'Well, how about this Peruvian mare's-nest of yours?'

'It's no mare's-nest,' I said; 'come and have a look at it.'

I took him upstairs into the library, and switched on the centre light and the reading-lamp on the writing-table. I gave him a chair at the table with his back to the fire, and fetched the papers I had been faking, out of the safe. He took them, and began to read them, poking over them in his short-sighted way, while I mended the fire. As soon as I saw his head in a favourable position I struck him heavily with the poker, just over the fourth cervical. It was delicate work calculating the exact force necessary to kill him without breaking the skin, but my professional experience was useful to me. He gave one loud gasp, and tumbled forward on to the table quite noiselessly. I put the poker back, and examined him. His neck was broken, and he was quite dead. I carried him into my bedroom and undressed him. It was about ten minutes to ten when I had finished. I put him away under my bed, which had been turned down for the night, and cleared up the papers in the library. Then I went downstairs, took Levy's umbrella, and let myself out at the hall door, shouting 'Good night' loudly enough to be heard in the basement if the servants should be listening. I walked briskly away down the street, went in by the hospital side door, and returned to the house noiselessly by way of the private passage. It would have been awkward if anybody had seen me then, but I leaned over the back stairs and heard the cook and her husband still talking in the kitchen. I slipped back into the hall, replaced the umbrella in the stand, cleared up my papers there, went up into the library and rang the bell. When the man appeared I told him to lock up everything except the private door to the hospital. I waited in the library until he had done so, and about 10.30 I heard both servants go up to bed. I waited a quarter of an hour longer and then went through to the dissecting-room. I wheeled one of the stretcher tables through the passage to the house door, and then went to fetch Levy. It was a nuisance having to get him downstairs, but I had not liked to make away with him in any of the ground-floor rooms, in case my servant should take a fancy to poke his head in during the few minutes that I was out of the house, or while locking up. Besides, that was a flea-bite to what I should have to do later. I put Levy on the table, wheeled him across to the hospital and substituted him for my interesting pauper. I was sorry to have to abandon the idea of getting a look at the latter's brain, but I could not afford to incur suspicion. It was still rather early, so I knocked down a few minutes getting

231

Levy ready for dissection. Then I put my pauper on the table and trundled him over to the house. It was now five past eleven, and I thought I might conclude that the servants were in bed. I carried the body into my bedroom. He was rather heavy, but less so than Levy, and my Alpine experience had taught me how to handle bodies. It is as much a matter of knack as of strength, and I am, in any case, a powerful man for my height. I put the body into the bed — not that I expected anyone to look in during my absence, but if they should they might just as well see me apparently asleep in bed. I drew the clothes a little over his head, stripped, and put on Levy's clothes, which were fortunately a little big for me everywhere, not forgetting to take his spectacles, watch and other oddments. At a little before half-past eleven I was in the road looking for a cab. People were just beginning to come home from the theatre, and I easily secured one at the corner of Prince of Wales Road. I told the man to drive me to Hyde Park Corner. There I got out, tipped him well, and asked him to pick me up again at the same place in an hour's time. He assented with an understanding grin, and I walked on up Park Lane. I had my own clothes with me in a suitcase, and carried my own overcoat and Levy's umbrella. When I got to No. 9 A there were lights in some of the top windows. I was very nearly too early, owing to the old man's having sent the servants to the theatre. I waited about for a few minutes, and heard it strike the quarter-past midnight. The lights were extinguished shortly after, and I let myself in with Levy's key.

It had been my original intention, when I thought over this plan of murder, to let Levy disappear from the study or the dining-room, leaving only a heap of clothes on the hearthrug. The accident of my having been able to secure Lady Levy's absence from London, however, made possible a solution more misleading, though less pleasantly fantastic. I turned on the hall light, hung up Levy's wet overcoat and placed his umbrella in the stand. I walked up noisily and heavily to the bedroom and turned off the light by the duplicate switch on the landing. I knew the house well enough, of course. There was no chance of my running into the manservant. Old Levy was a simple old man, who liked doing things for himself. He gave his valet little work, and never required any attendance at night. In the bedroom I took off Levy's gloves and put on a surgical pair, so as to leave no tell-tale finger-prints. As I wished to convey the impression that Levy had gone to bed in the usual way, I simply went to bed. The surest and simplest method of making a thing appear to have been done is to do it. A bed that has been rumpled about with one's hands, for instance, never looks like a bed that has been slept in. I dared not use Levy's brush, of course, as my hair is not of his colour, but I did everything else. I supposed that a thoughtful old man like Levy would put his boots handy for his valet, and I ought to have deduced that he would fold up his clothes. That was a mistake, but not an important one. Remembering that well-thought-out little work of Mr Bentley's, I had examined Levy's mouth for false teeth, but he had none. I did not forget, however, to wet his tooth-brush.

At one o'clock I got up and dressed in my own clothes by the light of my own pocket torch. I dared not turn on the bedroom lights, as there were light blinds to the windows. I put on my own boots and an old pair of goloshes outside the door. There was a thick Turkey carpet on the stairs and hall-floor, and I was not afraid of leaving marks. I hesitated whether to chance the banging of the front door, but decided it would be safer to take the latchkey. (It is now in the Thames. I dropped it over Battersea Bridge the next day.) I slipped quietly down, and listened for a few minutes with my ear to the letterbox. I heard a constable tramp past. As soon as his steps had died away in the distance I stepped out and pulled the door gingerly to. It closed almost soundlessly, and I walked away to pick up my cab. I had an overcoat of much the same pattern as Levy's, and had taken the precaution to pack an opera hat in my suitcase. I hoped the man would not notice that I had no umbrella this time. Fortunately the rain had diminished for the moment to a sort of drizzle, and if he noticed anything he made no observation. I told him to stop at 50 Overstrand Mansions, and I paid him off there, and stood under the porch till he had driven away. Then I hurried round to my own side door and let myself in. It was about a quarter to two, and the harder part of my task still lay before me.

My first step was so to alter the appearance of my subject as to eliminate any immediate suggestion either of Levy or of the workhouse vagrant. A fairly superficial alteration was all I considered necessary, since there was not likely to be any hue-and-cry after the pauper. He was fairly accounted for, and his deputy was at hand to represent him. Nor, if Levy was after all traced to my house would it be difficult to show that the body in evidence was, as a matter of fact, not his. A clean shave and a little hair-oiling and manicuring seemed sufficient to suggest a distinct personality for my silent accomplice. His hands had been well washed in hospital and, though calloused, were not grimy. I was not able to do the work as thoroughly as I should have liked, because time was getting on. I was not sure how long it would take me to dispose of him, and moreover, I feared the onset of *rigor mortis*, which would make my task more difficult. When I had him barbered to my satisfaction, I fetched a strong sheet and a couple of wide roller bandages, and fastened him up carefully, padding him with cotton wool wherever the bandages might chafe or leave a bruise.

Now came the really ticklish part of the business. I had already decided in my own mind that the only way of conveying him from the house was by the roof. To go through the garden at the back in this soft wet weather was to leave a ruinous trail behind us. To carry a dead man down a suburban street in the middle of the night seemed outside the range of practical politics. On the roof, on the other hand, the rain, which would have betrayed me on the ground, would stand my friend.

To reach the roof, it was necessary to carry my burden to the top of the house, past the servants' room, and hoist him out through the trapdoor in the box-room roof. Had it merely been a question of going quietly up there myself, I should have had no fear of waking the servants, but to do so burdened by a heavy body was more difficult. It would be possible, provided that the man and his wife were soundly asleep, but if not, the lumbering tread on the narrow stair and the noise of opening the trapdoor would be only too plainly audible. I tiptoed delicately up the stair and listened at their door. To my disgust I heard the man give a grunt and mutter something as he moved in his bed.

I looked at my watch. My preparations had taken nearly an hour, first and last, and I dared not be too late on the roof. I determined to take a bold step and, as it were, bluff out an alibi. I went without precaution against noise into the bathroom, turned on the hot and cold water taps to the full and pulled out the plug.

My household had often had occasion to complain of my habit of using the bath at irregular night hours. Not only does the rush of water into the cistern disturb any sleepers on the Prince of Wales Road side of the house, but my cistern is afflicted with peculiarly loud gurglings and thumpings, while frequently the pipes emit a loud groaning sound. To my delight, on this particular occasion, the cistern was in excellent form, honking, whistling and booming like a railway terminus. I gave the noise five minutes' start, and when I calculated that the sleepers would have finished cursing me and put their heads under the clothes to shut out the din, I reduced the flow of water to a small stream and left the bathroom, taking good care to leave the light burning and lock the door after me. Then I picked up my pauper and carried him upstairs as lightly as possible.

The box-room is a small attic on the side of the landing opposite the servants' bedroom and the cistern-room. It has a trapdoor, reached by a short, wooden

237

ladder. I set this up, hoisted up my pauper and climbed up after him. The water was still racing into the cistern, which was making a noise as though it were trying to digest an iron chain, and with the reduced flow in the bathroom the groaning of the pipes had risen almost to a hoot. I was not afraid of anybody hearing other noises. I pulled the ladder through on to the roof after me.

Between my house and the last house in Queen Caroline Mansions there is a space of only a few feet. Indeed, when the Mansions were put up, I believe there was some trouble about ancient lights, but I suppose the parties compromised somehow. Anyhow, my seven-foot ladder reached well across. I tied the body firmly to the ladder, and pushed it over till the far end was resting on the parapet of the opposite house. Then I took a short run across the cistern-room and the box-room roof, and landed easily on the other side, the parapet being happily both low and narrow.

The rest was simple. I carried my pauper along the flat roofs, intending to leave him, like the hunchback in the story, on someone's staircase or down a chimney. I had got about half-way along when I suddenly thought, 'Why, this must be about little Thipps's place,' and I remembered his silly face, and his silly chatter about vivisection. It occurred to me pleasantly how delightful it would be to deposit my parcel with him and see what he made of it. I lay down and peered over the parapet at the back. It was pitch-dark and pouring with rain again by this time, and I risked using my torch. That was the only incautious thing I did, and the odds against being seen from the houses opposite were long enough. One second's flash showed me what I hardly dared to hope — an open window just below me.

I knew those flats well enough to be sure it was either the bathroom or the kitchen. I made a noose in a third bandage that I had brought with me, and made it fast under the arms of the corpse. I twisted it into a double rope, and secured the end to the iron stanchion of a chimney-stack. Then I dangled our friend over. I went down after him myself with the aid of a drainpipe and was soon hauling him in by Thipps's bathroom window.

By that time I had got a little conceited with myself, and spared a few minutes to lay him out prettily and make him shipshape. A sudden inspiration suggested that I should give him the pair of pince-nez which I had happened to pick up at Victoria. I came across them in my pocket while I was looking for a penknife to loosen a knot, and I saw what distinction they would lend his appearance, besides making it more misleading. I fixed them on him, effaced all traces of my presence as far as possible, and departed as

I had come, going easily up between the drainpipe and the rope.

I walked quietly back, re-crossed my crevasse and carried in my ladder and sheet. My discreet accomplice greeted me with a reassuring gurgle and thump. I didn't make a sound on the stairs. Seeing that I had now been having a bath for about three-quarters of an hour, I turned the water off, and enabled my deserving domestics to get a little sleep. I also felt it was time I had a little myself.

First, however, I had to go over to the hospital and make all safe there. I took off Levy's head, and started to open up the face. In twenty minutes his own wife could not have recognised him. I returned, leaving my wet goloshes and mackintosh by the garden door. My trousers I dried by the gas-stove in my bedroom, and brushed away all traces of mud and brickdust. My pauper's beard I burned in the library.

I got a good two hours' sleep from five to seven, when my man called me as usual. I apologised for having kept the water running so long and so late, and added that I thought I would have the cistern seen to.

I was interested to note that I was rather extra hungry at breakfast, showing that my night's work had caused a certain wear-and-tear of tissue. I went over afterwards to continue my dissection. During the morning a peculiarly thick-headed police inspector came to inquire whether a body had escaped from the hospital. I had him brought to me where I was, and had the pleasure of showing him the work I was doing on Sir Reuben Levy's head. Afterwards I went round with him to Thipps's and was able to satisfy myself that my pauper looked very convincing.

As soon as the Stock Exchange opened I telephoned my various brokers, and by exercising a little care, was able to sell out the greater part of my Peruvian stock on a rising market. Towards the end of the day, however, buyers became rather unsettled as a result of Levy's death, and in the end I did not make more than a few hundreds by the transaction.

Trusting I have now made clear to you any point which you may have found obscure and with congratulations on the good fortune and perspicacity which have enabled you to defeat me, I remain, with kind remembrances to your mother,

Yours very truly,

JULIAN FREKE,

Post-Scriptum: My will is made, leaving my money to St Luke's Hospital, and bequeathing my body to the same institution for dissection. I feel sure that my brain will be of interest to the scientific world. As I shall die by my own hand, I imagine that there may be a little difficulty about this. Will you do me a favour, if you can, of seeing the persons concerned in the inquest, and obtaining that the brain is not damaged by an unskilful practitioner at the post-mortem, and that the body is disposed of according to my wish?

By the way, it may be of interest to you to know that I appreciated your motive in calling this afternoon. It conveyed a warning, and I am acting upon it. In spite of the disastrous consequences to myself, I was pleased to realise that you had not underestimated my nerve and intelligence, and refused the injection. Had you submitted to it, you would, of course, never reached home alive. No trace would have been left in your body of the injection, which consisted of a harmless preparation of strychnine, mixed with an almost unknown poison, for which there is at present no recognised test, a concentrated solution of sn —

At this point the manuscript broke off.

'Well, that's all clear enough,' said Parker.

'Isn't it queer?' said Lord Peter. 'All that coolness, all those brains — and then he couldn't resist writing a confession to show how clever he was, even to keep his head out of the noose.'

'And a very good thing for us,' said Inspector Sugg, 'but Lord bless you, sir, these criminals are all alike.'

'Freke's epitaph,' said Parker, when the Inspector had departed. 'What next, Peter?'

'I shall now give a dinner party,' said Lord Peter, 'to Mr John P. Milligan and his secretary and to Messrs Crimplesham and Wicks. I feel

242

they deserve it for not having murdered Levy.'

'Well, don't forget the Thippses,' said Mr Parker.

'On no account,' said Lord Peter, 'would I deprive myself of the pleasure of Mrs Thipps's company. Bunter!'

'My lord?'

'The Napoleon brandy.'

WIMSEY, PETER DEATH BREDON, D.S.O.; *born* 1890, *2nd son of* Mortimer Gerald Bredon Wimsey, 15th Duke of Denver, and of Honoria Lucasta, *daughter of* Francis Delagardie of Bellingham Manor, Hants.

Educated: Eton College and Balliol College, Oxford (1st class honours, Sch. of Mod. Hist. 1912); served with H.M. Forces 1914/18 (Major, Rifle Brigade). *Author of:* 'Notes on the Collecting of Incunabula', 'The Murderer's Vade-Mecum', etc. *Recreations:* Criminology; bibliophily; music; cricket.

Clubs: Marlborough; Egotists'. *Residences:* 110A Piccadilly, W.; Bredon Hall, Duke's Denver, Norfolk.

Arms: Sable, 3 mice courant, argent; crest, a domestic cat couched as to spring, proper; motto: As my Whimsy takes me.

This Re-Issue Of
Whose Body?

(which has received *some corrections* and *amendments* from MISS SAYERS) has for a postscript *a short biography of Lord Peter Wimsey,* brought up to date (May 1935) and communicated by his uncle PAUL AUSTIN DELAGARDIE.

I am asked by Miss Sayers to fill up certain lacunae and correct a few trifling errors of fact in her account of my nephew Peter's career. I shall do so with pleasure. To appear publicly in print is every man's ambition, and by acting as a kind of running footman to my nephew's triumph I shall only be showing a modesty suitable to my advanced age.

The Wimsey family is an ancient one — too ancient, if you ask me. The only sensible thing Peter's father ever did was to ally his exhausted stock with the vigorous French-English strain of the Delagardies. Even so, my nephew Gerald (the present Duke of Denver) is nothing but a beef-witted English squire, and my niece Mary was flighty and foolish enough till she married a policeman and settled down. Peter, I am glad to say, takes after his mother and me. True, he is all nerves and nose — but that is better than being all brawn and no brains like his father and brothers, or a mere bundle of emotions, like Gerald's boy, Saint-George. He has at least inherited the Delagardie brains, by way of safeguard to the unfortunate Wimsey temperament.

Peter was born in 1890. His mother was being very much worried at the time by her husband's behaviour (Denver was always tiresome, though the big scandal did not break out till the Jubilee year), and her anxieties may have affected the boy. He was a colourless shrimp of a child, very restless and mischievous, and always much too sharp for his age. He had nothing of Gerald's robust physical beauty, but he developed what I can best call a kind of bodily cleverness, more skill than strength. He had a quick eye for a ball and beautiful hands for a horse. He had the devil's own pluck, too: the intelligent sort of pluck that sees the risk before it takes it. He suffered badly from nightmares as a child. To his father's consternation he grew up with a passion for books and music.

His early schooldays were not happy. He was a fastidious child, and I suppose it was natural that his school-fellows should call him 'Flimsy' and treat him as a kind of comic turn. And he might, in sheer self-protection, have accepted the position and degenerated into a mere licensed buffoon, if some games-master at Eton had not discovered that he was a brilliant natural cricketer. After that, of course, all his eccentricities were accepted as wit, and Gerald underwent the salutary shock of seeing his despised younger brother become a bigger personality than himself. By the time he reached the Sixth Form, Peter had contrived to become the fashion — athlete, scholar, *arbiter elegantiarum* — *nec pluribus impar*. Cricket had a great deal to do with it — plenty of Eton men will remember the 'Great Flim' and his performance against Harrow — but I take credit to myself for introducing him to a good tailor, showing him the way about Town, and teaching him to distinguish good wine from bad. Denver bothered little about him — he had too many entanglements of his own and in addition was taken up with Gerald, who by this time was making a prize fool of himself at Oxford. As a matter of fact Peter never got on with his father, he was a ruthless young critic of the paternal misdemeanours, and his sympathy for his mother had a destructive effect upon his sense of humour.

Denver, needless to say, was the last person to tolerate his own failings in his offspring. It cost him a good deal of money to extricate Gerald from the Oxford affair, and he was willing enough to turn his other son over to me. Indeed at the age of seventeen, Peter came to me of his own accord. He was old for his age and exceedingly reasonable, and I treated him as a man of the world. I established him in trustworthy hands in Paris, instructing him to keep his affairs upon a sound business footing and to see that they terminated with goodwill on both sides and generosity on his. He fully justified my confidence. I believe that no woman has ever found cause to complain of Peter's treatment; and two at least of them have since married royalty (rather obscure royalties, I admit, but royalty of a sort). Here again, I insist upon my due share of the credit; however good the material one has to work upon it is ridiculous to leave any young man's social education to chance.

The Peter of this period was really charming, very frank, modest and well-mannered, with a pretty, lively wit. In 1909 he went up with a scholarship to read History at Balliol, and here, I must confess, he became rather intolerable. The world was at his feet, and he began to give himself airs. He acquired affectations, an exaggerated Oxford manner and a monocle, and aired his opinions a good deal, both in and out of the Union, though I will do him the justice to say that he never attempted to patronise his mother or me. He was in his second year when Denver broke his neck out hunting and Gerald succeeded to the title. Gerald showed more sense of responsibility than I had expected in dealing with the estate; his worst mistake was to marry his cousin Helen, a scrawny, over-bred prude, all county from head to heel. She and Peter loathed each other cordially; but he could always take refuge with his mother at the Dower House.

And then, in his last year at Oxford, Peter fell in love with a child of seventeen and instantly forgot everything he had ever been taught. He treated that girl as if she was made of gossamer, and me as a hardened old monster of depravity who had made him unfit to touch her delicate purity. I won't deny that they made an exquisite pair — all white and gold — a prince and a princess of moonlight, people said. Moonshine would have been nearer the mark. What Peter was to do in twenty years' time with a wife who had neither brains nor character nobody but his mother and myself ever troubled to ask, and he, of course, was completely besotted. Happily, Barbara's parents decided that she was too young to marry; so Peter went in for his final Schools in the temper of a Sir Eglamore achieving his first dragon; laid his First-Class Honours at his lady's feet like the dragon's head, and settled down to a period of virtuous probation.

Then came the War. Of course the young idiot was mad to get married before he went. But his own honourable scruples made him mere wax in other people's hands. It was pointed out to him that if he came back mutilated it would be very unfair to the girl. He hadn't thought of that, and rushed off in a frenzy of self-abnegation to release her from the engagement. I had no hand in that; I was glad enough of the result, but I couldn't stomach the means.

He did very well in France, he made a good officer and the men liked him. And then, if you please, he came back on leave with his captaincy in '16, to find the girl married — to a hardbitten rake of a Major Somebody, whom she had nursed in the V.A.D. hospital, and whose motto with women was catch 'em quick and treat 'em rough. It was pretty brutal; for the girl hadn't had the nerve to tell Peter beforehand. They got married in a hurry when they heard he was coming home, and all he got on landing was a letter, announcing the *fait accompli* and reminding him that he had set her free himself.

I will say for Peter that he came straight to me and admitted that he had been a fool. 'All right,' said I, 'you've had your lesson. Don't go and make a fool of yourself in the other direction.' So he went back to his job with (I am sure) the fixed intention of getting killed; but all he got was his majority and his D.S.O. for some recklessly good intelligence work behind the German front. In 1918 he was blown up and buried in a shell-hole near Caudry, and that left him with a bad nervous breakdown, lasting, on and off, for two years. After that, he set himself up in a flat in Piccadilly, with the man Bunter (who had been his sergeant and was, and is, devoted to him), and started out to put himself together again.

I don't mind saying that I was prepared for almost anything. He had lost all of his beautiful frankness, he shut everybody out of his confidence, including his mother and me, adopted an impenetrable frivolity of manner and a dilettante pose, and became, in fact, the complete comedian. He was wealthy and could do as he chose, and it gave me a certain amount of sardonic entertainment to watch the efforts of post-war feminine London to capture him. 'It can't,' said one solicitous matron, 'be good for poor Peter to live like a hermit.' 'Madame,' said I, 'if he did, it wouldn't be.' No; from that point of view he gave me no anxiety. But I could not but think it dangerous that a man of his ability should have no job to occupy his mind, and I told him so.

In 1921 came the business of the Attenbury Emeralds. That affair has never been written up, but it made a good deal of noise, even at that noisiest of periods. The trial of the thief was a series of red-hot sensations, and the biggest sensation of the bunch was when Lord Peter Wimsey walked into the witness-box as chief witness for the prosecution.

That was notoriety with a vengeance. Actually, to an experienced intelligence officer, I don't suppose the investigation had offered any great difficulties; but a 'noble sleuth' was something new in thrills. Denver was furious; personally, I didn't mind what Peter did, provided he did something. I thought he seemed happier for the work, and I liked the Scotland Yard man he had picked up during the run of the case. Charles Parker is a quiet, sensible, well-bred fellow, and has been a good friend and brother-in-law to Peter. He has the valuable quality of being fond of people without wanting to turn them inside out.

The only trouble about Peter's new hobby was that it had to be more than a hobby, if it was to be any hobby for a gentleman. You cannot get murderers hanged for your private entertainment. Peter's intellect pulled him one way and his nerves another, till I began to be afraid they would pull him to pieces. At the end of every case we had the old nightmares and shell-shock over again. And then Denver, of all people — Denver, the crashing great booby, in the middle of his fulminations against Peter's degrading and notorious police activities, must needs get himself indicted on a murder charge and stand his trial in the House of Lords, amid a blaze of publicity which made all Peter's efforts in that direction look like damp squibs.

Peter pulled his brother out of that mess, and, to my relief, was human enough to get drunk on the strength of it. He now admits that his 'hobby' is his legitimate work for society, and has developed sufficient interest in public affairs to undertake small diplomatic jobs from time to time under the Foreign Office. Of late he has become a little more ready to show his feelings, and a little less terrified of having any to show.

His latest eccentricity has been to fall in love with that girl whom he cleared of the charge of poisoning her lover. She refused to marry him, as any woman of character would. Gratitude and a humiliating inferiority complex are no foundation for matrimony; the position was false from the start. Peter had the sense, this time, to take my advice. 'My boy,' I said, 'what was wrong for you twenty years back is right now. It's not the innocent young things that need gentle handling — it's the ones that have been frightened and hurt. Begin again from the beginning — but I warn you that you will need all the self-discipline you have ever learnt.'

Well, he has tried. I don't think I have ever seen such patience. The girl has brains and character and honesty; but he has got to teach her how to take, which is far more difficult than learning to give. I think they will find one another, if they can keep their passions from running ahead of their wills. He does realise, I know, that in this case there can be no consent but free consent.

Peter is forty-five now, it is really time he was settled. As you will see, I have been one of the important formative influences in his career, and, on the whole, I feel he does me credit. He is a true Delagardie, with little of the Wimseys about him except (I must be fair) that underlying sense of social responsibility which prevents the English landed gentry from being a total loss, spiritually speaking. Detective or no detective, he is a scholar and a gentleman; it will amuse me to see what sort of shot he makes at being a husband and father. I am getting an old man, and have no son of my own (that I know of); I should be glad to see Peter happy. But as his mother says, 'Peter has always had everything except the things he really wanted,' and I suppose he is luckier than most.

PAUL AUSTIN DELAGARDIE